THE SLEDGE CHRONICLES

THE SLEDGE CHRONICLES:

ROCK STAR HITMAN

BY: DAVID ELLEFSON
&
DREW FORTIER

Cover art layout design by: Melody Myers
David Ellefson author photo by: Melody Myers
Drew Fortier author photo by: Tharasa DiMeo
First Edition: September 2020
Printed in the United States of America
ISBN: 978-1-7353796-1-6

David Ellefson & Drew Fortier would like to thank: Thom Hazaert, Melody Myers, Tharasa DiMeo, Richard Easterling, Vin Dombroski, and Robert Spector.

1

NOT BAD FOR A FARM BOY

MY NAME IS SLEDGE and I grew up in a stereotypical main street type Midwest town in Iowa called Delane. It was a pleasant sort of place with honest, decent, and hardworking people; born of the fabric, which bears goodness and a nice little place to retire later in life.

The problem was, it wasn't for me; best of all, it was a simple life I knew before I was on "The Grid".

Growing up in a small Midwestern town was nice. And by nice, I mean just that:

Nice.

Nothing horrible, nothing too exciting, just nice and pleasant; which is fine for most people.

I have an acronym for it:

Nothing

Interesting or

Certainly

Exciting
N.I.C.E.

As I said, my name is Sledge but my real name is Toby MacCready. The most un-rock n' roll name in the world, so I did the most logical thing; I changed it. Or should I say, as a budding teenager and through a series of ironic situations, my coworkers nicknamed me, then of course my friends and band mates made it stick. They thought it sounded cool. Anything sounded cooler than Toby MacCready so I was totally fine with that.

I needed to get away from my "Midwest Nice" reputation and "Sledge" definitely had more of an edge to it than "Toby".

For instance,

"Hey Sledge! Look! There's some hot trim over there at the bar! Let's go get it!"

VS.

"Toby, will you go fetch a gallon of milk from the grocery store?"

Or:

"Yo Sledge! Killer show tonight, man!"

VS.

"Toby, did you do your chores?"

See what I mean?

Sledge Seether is what my full "name" turned out to be. It became official on behalf of The Agency. It amazes me what people would do for fortune and fame. It amazes me what I did and have done and am doing for fortune and fame, but we'll get to all that in a bit.

As a youngster, I always had a yearning for something bigger and more exciting outside the box of life in Delane. I didn't really know what I was looking for, but I was always on the search for it.

Although I could back it up, I was never a mean, malicious or devilish kind of guy; but I always had a sort of wanderlust hard wired inside of me, a lusting which always led my interests into interesting scenarios and often into the abyss.

With that said, my whole love affair with music began the first time I heard Led Zeppelin's "Whole Lotta Love" on the radio. I was about 12 and it absolutely blew my mind and stimulated me in every way possible. It made me feel like I was listening to something I shouldn't be listening to. It was heavy, it was sexy, and it had an edge. I had never heard anything like it before and I needed to dive in and immerse myself.

So I did.

With living in a small farm town, there wasn't much around by way of music stores but I managed to save up enough money from my paper route for bus fare to grab a few albums from the closest record shop. I ended up coming home with Led Zeppelin II as well as Kiss Destroyer. I couldn't get enough of that music. It rang a bell inside of me that would not stop reverberating my soul.

As I dove deeper into high school life, I discovered more and more of the classics such as Rush, Cheap Trick, Kansas, Judas Priest, Black Sabbath, etc.

I then got to the point where listening to all these bands just simply was not enough. I needed to go a step further. I needed to be inside the music somehow; the same way the music was inside me.

Then it hit me.

I needed to be in a band.

I had to be in a band.

Plus, that would be my one-way ticket out of Delane, Iowa. Most people never got out of that town. People that were born there, died there. I didn't want that to be me. I needed to get out of there and music was the answer.

But first I needed to learn to play an instrument. There was no musical ability in my family whatsoever but that didn't affect me one bit. I knew that if I had a guitar in front of me that I would work it until my fingers bled; until I sounded like Jimmy Page.

I knew I had it in me.

There was no way I could afford a guitar with my paper route though so I needed to find something more lucrative. I inquired around town and it turned out that the local slaughterhouse was looking for people on a full-time basis.

I always heard that the man who ran the slaughterhouse, Mr. Goodman, was a complete hard ass ex-military type that was a stone's throw away from retirement and very hard to get along with. A very bottom-line kind of guy, if you will. Needless to say, I was nervous but knew that it was my only shot in Delane to make some real money to get out.

I rode my bike to the slaughterhouse and met with Mr. Goodman. The stench of stale death was very poignant in the air, which explained Mr. Goodman's perpetual grimace. He was tall and wide with a booming voice that was very intimidating. He definitely exceeded his reputation.

"What experience do you have, young man?" he asked.

Even with that logical inquiry, his voice made me feel like I had done something wrong. I managed to let a few words fall out of my mouth,

"I had a paper route."

He just stared at me for a long moment. Stone faced. I didn't know what to do so I just started humming "In-A-Gadda-Da-Vida" for some damn reason. It had been stuck in my head all day.

"Iron Butterfly?" bellowed Mr. Goodman.

Another tense moment passed as I kept on humming. Then Mr. Goodman's whole demeanor changed,

"I remember getting laid to that song in the 60's. Good shit, young man. You're hired. You start Monday."

I couldn't believe it. I got the job. Monday would be one step closer to making my rock star dreams realized.

It took a long while to get used to everything about working at that slaughterhouse. The smell, the people, the blood, the gore, etc. But you know how they say everything happens for a reason? Then I guess you could also say that what I learned working at that place equipped me with a certain set of skills that came in handy a little bit later on in life. You wouldn't believe me if I told you but as I said before, we'll get to that.

My first day reeked of newbie innocence. It was my job to put the cow to sleep, if you will, and I had to do it with a sledgehammer.

"Have at it boy," my co-worker barked at me as he handed me the sledgehammer.

"It's all a means for an end," he spat out.

I took a moment to compose myself and I then made my first mistake. I looked into the cow's eye. We made a connection. It was aware of me, and I was aware of it.

For some reason, in my head, I immediately gave the cow a name, Grace. I humanized the cow and in a split second my conscious came up with a back-story for her and everything.

She was a single mom just doing what she had to do to raise her calves. Just making an honest living bringing up her babies. But the next thing she knew, she was inside of some strange barn with all these people staring at her. All she could think about was where her babies were. She was worried sick and stunned with concern.

"We don't got all fucking day, boy!" my co-worker sternly scolded toward me, which made me wince.

Grace then gave me a look of concern. Dread washed over me. She was a living creature for god's sake! I took a deep breath and suddenly all I could think about was being on stage with my guitar hung low and thousands of screaming fans begging for more; that was worth more than anything to me. The job was just a stepping-stone to greatness. I needed it.

"If you don't kill this heffer within the next 5 seconds, we will replace you with someone who will!" threatened my co-worker.

I then picked up the sledgehammer, lifted it over my right shoulder, closed my eyes and with all my might struck Grace in the head with a downward blow as hard as I could. All I could hear immediately after the thunderous explosion of hammer meeting skull was pure silence.

I opened my eyes and looked down. All that was left of Grace's head was pulp and brain matter. Blood was shooting out in a perpetual fountain. She was obliterated.

"Damn boy! You wanted that cow dead and you fuckin' nailed 'er!" praised my co-worker.

He continued, "Awright now, Sledge, ready for the next one?"

All I could think about was playing to a packed-out amphitheater and changing people's lives with my music. I looked at him dead in the eye and said, "Let's do this."

To be honest with you, as terrible as I felt, I kind of liked it. I didn't have a choice but to like it. Not to mention, after my first day, everyone kept on calling me "Sledge" and I was completely okay with that. It was leagues better than Toby anyway.

As the month's passed by, I was finally able to save up enough from the slaughterhouse to afford an instrument. I found an electric guitar and amplifier in a local ad. I loved everything about it; it was thin, bright colored and to me it screamed major cool factor.

I saw a few older buddies at school trying to play the guitar because they thought it would bring them the girls. I was really too young to even understand girls at that point in my life, and any interactions up until then were just a few love notes and innocent kisses on the playground or by the lockers in the school hallways. But this guitar suddenly propelled the idea of me becoming something much bigger, much cooler.

As soon as I got the guitar, things changed. Jason Verset was a high school bully who would taunt me on the way to school. He would tease me and call me his favorite nickname of "Mcsewer". Usually I would time my walk to school just to avoid him and the inevitable "nuggies", snowballs to my face, and other demoralizing acts of pure hatred he would force upon me. But, after I got the guitar, even he responded with a new attitude.

"Hey Mcsewer, how's that guitar coming along? You ever gonna play for us?" he would ask.

While still taunting, it was a new attitude from him and one that quickly led to us talking about cool albums he owned and what he thought were the cool bands, like Ted Nugent, Cheap Trick, Kiss and more. Trust me, it was progress! It also didn't go unnoticed that if the guitar could affect some douche bag bully like Jason Verset, then it was probably a secret weapon of defense against other offenders toward me in life.

As for the girls, at first it was the notorious bad girls around town (the female equivalent to Jason Verset) who lent me their attention and wandering eyes, which was scary because they also had the hard-edged drop out type boyfriends, like Jason Verset, who had spent their lives in the high school principal offices; usually yielding a school suspension or expulsion.

Their sort of anti-social behavior often escalated them into juvenile delinquent centers, jails and the sorts. Fighting and violence were their middle names so when their women began to shower me with their approvals, I wasn't exactly thrilled, yet it was a beginning to my teenage testosterone exploits.

Eventually, the bad boys thought I was a pretty cool kid as well; all because of that guitar.

I began to see a devilish grin in the good girls of Delane; a sort of savage and untamed intent of deed frothing forward from them. Here were girls who seemed like puritans in the daytime, groomed to grow into the prim and proper ladies, like their mothers before them. Yet with that guitar in my hand, I was able to extract a sort of primal urge, which was a panty dropper, even they weren't anticipating.

Maybe just knowing I could do it was satisfaction enough and while not the leading motivation for my rock n roll impulses, it was one that satisfactorily lurked in the back of my mind.

My parents were generally supportive of my love of rock n roll and my aspirations to have some sort of career in the field. The only condition being that I kept my act together and maintain at least a B grade average.

My father was the town's local pharmacist at our family owned MacCready's Drug Store on Second Street and my mother was a nurse and homemaker to raise me and my sister Molly. She was a decent girl, one grade younger than me who kept good grades, dated a decent guy from high school and was overall pretty cool. She stayed focused on her life and me on mine.

As a family, we took weekend vacations during my school years and enjoyed a relatively pain free life devoid of any major tragedies. My mom and dad married in their mid-twenties and were young enough to enjoy raising our family in a youthful, yet stable family life in Delane.

I've grown up comfortable in an upper middle-class environment with a respect for work and making money, especially since I didn't have my sights set on the usual college and professional work path my father followed.

With that said, I continued to focus on being the greatest musician that I could be by developing my own feel, my own style, and my own

identity. It was only a matter of time before I was able to find some like-minded individuals to start something up and get the hell outta Dodge.
And I did.

2

ONE LIFE, ONE MISSION

FAST FORWARD A FEW years of digging in the trenches of the music scene and soaking up every piece of knowledge I could soak up from every situation imaginable. From learning how to handle being stiffed by a promoter through sheer unconditional violence, to knowing how to handle on stage faux-pas like your guitar strap breaking mid-song. Trust me, there was no cool way to recover from that one.

All you could do is take it in stride. I also learned to make sure you void your bladder before every gig. Let's just say I was thankful to be wearing black pants during one particular gig. Lessons learned.

With that said, let's face it; we all start at the same place, the bottom. It was especially true with a rock band. Some stay there, some move a few notches up the ladder and only the very select few (like .00003%) ever go anywhere with their ambitions, which you could actually call a career.

I've been playing in bands since I picked up the guitar at age 13 and I've seen enough to know that success in music is usually never just about someone's, talent. Rather it's about having that key X Factor, that something which makes you compelling enough to stand out from the crowd.

It also helps to have a bulldog manager to push through all of the other douchey people in a con-artist business. Barnum & Bailey were right; it's all just one big circus!

One day, I remember stopping by my usual haunt, that being Hans' Music Store on Main Street in Delane. A flyer caught my attention as I noticed there was a Battle of the Bands event coming up called Iowa Rock Fest and it was to take place over in Des Moines over Independence Day summer weekend. Even more interesting, I didn't recognize the promoter's name, and I was pretty familiar with who was active in the area from the big shows to the little guys.

While it promised some concessionary prizes like free gear, etc. I was more interested in the promise that the grand prize winner would be flown to LA to be contracted by an exclusive booking agent and possible record deal. Now this was the exposure I was looking for; for me and my band Villain.

Villain were a focused, tight knit four-piece band of dedicated musicians who spent every free moment rehearsing our songs for shows and recording opportunities. I was the lead singer and played rhythm guitar, Gus played lead guitar, Blake played bass and Slim was our drummer.

We were certainly young, but the music business was a young man's game, and in my opinion, with our dead set focus as a unit, and with a little professional grooming from the big boys out in a place like LA, I knew we would have a shot at something bigger. Not to be shrewd, but if for any reason these boys didn't want to take a stab at an opportunity like LA, then I planned to go at it alone.

As I've said before, I would seek the unknown and I knew that my place in life was on the big stage, so I would do anything it took to get there.

Exposure is always what you're looking for with any band and at that stage of our career it was more important than anything else. Ultimately, I had been trying to build a fan base with Villain for about a year and a half by that point; we formed during the summer before my sophomore year in high school. In fact, I had helped form every band I had been in around Delane.

While I sat in with a few musicians when I was just starting out, I quickly learned I wasn't a joiner per se. It has always been in my blood to be the impetus to start bands and get them off the ground.

I was also wise enough to know I couldn't do it all myself; that I needed a real manager, an agent, and eventually a record company to get me to where I needed to go.

Fortunately, I had the knack to write and sing my own songs, and to build the band around my ideas, which was a real plus and put me in the driver's seat. Bands are never really a democracy, as you have to have a leader. Villain was no different. I lead, and the other guys followed.

Our biggest challenge in Delane, was that we were in Podunk, Iowa; smack dab in the middle of country music fans, most being the local farmers. So, it was a tough uphill battle to get anywhere around there as a rock musician. But I aimed to make enough noise with Villain to anyone who would listen so I could build a buzz and get some attention from someone on the Coasts.

I said earlier, my goal was to get the hell outta Delane, either with or without Villain and the guys in the band knew it, too. It was my senior year of high school and it was the time to shit or get off the pot.

There was no way in hell I'd be working in a slaughterhouse, marrying a local girl, and settling down like everyone else did around those parts. My life was out 'there' somewhere playing music; anywhere really. Anywhere except Delane.

So, I called the promoter contact on the flyer hanging in Hans' music store and was hopeful to get Villain on the bill for that July. One thing I knew about show business was that reality becomes perception and if the perception is that you're getting big, that creates a buzz with the fans, and the concert promoters. Hopefully Iowa Rock Fest would be another notch up the ladder of success.

It was funny how a place like Hans' store was necessary to a local music scene, especially to connect with other musicians; the few of us in the area who actually understood music and all of its ups and downs.

Hans was the grandson of a German family who moved to the area from Europe in the late 1800's. After a few tours in the military, he had some regional success in the area as a trombone player in a jazz swing-band years back, and he then stayed active as accordionist in a local Polka band. While that doesn't sound super sexy by modern-day pop music standards, Hans knew how a musician thinks and he always understood me.

He'd say, "Kid, if you got the goods you'll know it by the way the audience responds when you're onstage. If you got it, you gotta go get it, and the sooner the better. The music business is for youngsters so go get 'em kid."

Hans and I had spent many afternoons dissecting the similarities of rock n roll against the progressive be-bop jazz music he grew up on. So, for me, his store was the only place for a musician like me to find some type of hang out away from the real world.

That store was where I met the other three guys in Villain as they would come and go after school on the weekends to buy records and most of their gear. Unless we were willing to drive 75 minutes over to Des Moines or an hour up to Cedar Rapids, it was the only game in town for a music hangout.

Small towns are as much known for their liquor & drug consumption as anything; with the youth usually citing that there was nothing else to do as the main offense.

Fortunately, I never really fell into that apart from a few beers here and there at a weekend party. Our motivations were pure and Villain was about playing gigs whenever we could. Plus, we weren't old enough to hang around the bars, which pushed us to find every opportunity we could to play out.

We had a couple local guys over 21 years of age who pitched in as our crew from time to time, and they were happy to vouch for us to be in the bars when the show opportunities arose, but that meant playing cover songs which just made you a cover band, not an original band vying for a recording career.

Fortunately, for me, partying was something I only did when bored or looking to hang a bit, never as a primary lifestyle. Beer and girls were the accessories, not the main attraction in my life at that point. But as a musician, the booze and girls were always around so I kept a close eye on my band guys and any outsiders who might be trying to get too close to distract us from the singular focus of stardom. Fortunately, except our drummer Slim, our band had little hassles with the girls or commitments to our good work ethic. But, as popularity rises, so do the temptations and distractions.

By that point we were rehearsing our asses off in hopes to get a spot on the Iowa Rock Fest. We had our fingers crossed so tight that they bled.

3

MAKE IT OR BREAK IT

NO MORE THAN 48 hours after I made contact with the promoter of the Iowa Rock Fest (dubbed IRF for short) I received a phone call from a guy who claimed to be a promoter representative named Robert DiAngelis. He told me he had checked out Villain's press kit and loved what he heard and saw.

He said, "Looks like you boys have been working hard around there. You're a little young, but we'd like to offer you a slot at the festival."

"There are some pretty big national acts on the bill, but our side stage is designed to give a couple young bands a good look, and maybe even a little break."

"You know there is a Grand Prize winner and that artist or band will be flown out to LA to be connected with the big boys. I'll have my assistant send you more information. Welcome aboard the festival; it's gonna be one hell of an event for the summer!"

Shortly thereafter, I received a call from Robert's assistant Jane. She gave us all the pertinent information on the festival including set times, set length, production contacts, how many guests we could have and everything.

We were offered a modest $200 stipend from the festival and it was made very clear that with many bands performing each day of the three-day event that we could not go over our designated set length or we would be forced to forfeit our stipend.

As soon as I told the boys in the band, our energy had shot to a whole new level. These were the type of shows that would give us major exposure in front of a lot of potential fans. Even though our set time was 30 minutes long and designated to be at 2pm on a Friday, the first day of the festival, there would probably be close to 5000 early concertgoers in attendance.

The few weeks leading up to the festival was major prep time for us to rehearse our songs and tighten up our show. While we weren't allowed to use any pyro technics or other enhancements, we did have some staging boxes and drum riser ramps that allowed for us to run around the stage and have a more three-dimensional look to our show.

While I was center stage singing most of the time, I also learned from other big arena rock bands that moving to various microphones placed on select locations on the stage helped give an advantage to me being more active during our show.

Our lead guitar player Gus was stoked and immediately began working on a short but spectacular featured solo. Gus was a decent looking guy who took his guitar playing very seriously. His girlfriend Tracee was a good-looking girl who too often weighed in her opinion on the band, which always pissed me off. I had many discussions with Gus to stop letting her interfere with the band and my vision.

While my urgings were well received early on, I got the feeling that since we were in our senior year of high school, she could easily coerce him into staying behind in Delane with her, rather than pursuing his talents in a big-time band.

It was a shame because he had the potential to really go somewhere, but in my mind, what separated the boys from the men were those who got pussy whipped and those of us who stayed the course to fulfill our mission of global domination. As I said, I knew my destiny, and if Gus was part of it, great. If not, then I would move on and it would be his loss, not mine.

Slim was an energetic guy and like a lot of drummers, seemed content to just be hitting his drums and always looked forward to the thrill of being onstage. He looked and played decent, but I was always on him about practicing more.

While he wasn't pussy whipped over one girl in particular, he was always on the prowl for any girl in general. God love him for his love of girls and rock n roll, but it was usually to the detriment of his playing.

One time while we were in the studio cutting a few demo tracks, our engineer warned us of Slim's inability to play to a click track, and mentioned that as bigger opportunities came our way that Slim shouldn't be surprised when a producer eventually brings in a replacement drummer to play his parts on a recording.

It shocked Slim, probably mostly from us as his friends and our loyalty to him, but the message was clear; everyone was replaceable except the one who wrote the songs, which was me.

Our bass player Blake was a chill dude and we figured he would probably go off to pursue his college career at Marquette University in Milwaukee after his high school graduation which was urged by his father of the same alma mater so for the time being, he fit just fine and didn't cause any waves.

The only obstacle in front of us before the show was our high school graduation and all the bullshit that would go along with that, mostly with our families up our ass about grades, future plans, college admission forms, and the like.

Fortunately, for me, my family knew I was getting out of Delane after high school, the following fall anyway, but still the inevitable questions fired my way of,

"Where are you going next year anyway?"

As well as, "Are you really going to try and make a go of this rock n roll career thing? You do know most people don't make it, right?"

I didn't care, I knew my destiny and at that moment, I had a good hunch that something big was about to happen. I had a feeling about that festival and when I trusted my gut, things usually worked out well. At least they had up to that point.

At rehearsal the night before the big show, after slamming through our set for the festival, I stood in front of my band to mentally prepare them for what was in store,

"Guys, we've all come a long way here. We survived high school together as a band. We survived endless gigs for no money as a band. We even survived Slim's mom's cooking as a band."

With the nervousness in the air for the following day's show, everybody was very appreciative of that glimmer of levity. I then continued,

"But as we are dipping our toes into the great unknown that is called life, we are now all at a fork in the road. What we need to understand is-"

Gus' girlfriend, Tracee, then interrupted me,

"Sledge, how long is this going to go on for? Because me and Gussy have dinner reservations and-"

At that point I had had enough of that broad always trying to ruin any kind of band situation. Without ever making eye contact with her, I shot a glare directly over to Gus and said,

"Dude, could we please kick Tracee out of here for once? Just once? With all that's going on here and with everything at stake, you damn well know as well as the rest of us that this could be our last few days with this line up of the band, so let's try and at least sink into whatever kind of camaraderie we have left here, cool?"

Gus nodded and looked over to Tracee,

"Babe, go wait in the car."

She shot back a glare that straight up said that Gus was in the doghouse and not getting laid for at least a week. She huffed and puffed her way out of the room and we all let out a sigh of relief, even Gus. I then continued my speech for my boys,

32

"As I was saying, we don't know what's going to happen tomorrow. Hell, we don't know what could happen in five minutes. But all I know is that we are primed and ready to absolutely obliterate the competition tomorrow."

"No matter what happens, just know I'm glad it was with you guys. I know you all have separate plans in life aside from my vision of a band, but I am forever thankful for your dedication and hard work."

"We have all graduated high school, but at the same time we are about to graduate as a band. Tomorrow is Villain's graduation. With that said, let's get some rest and- "

I dramatically paused in that very moment. My bandmates were staring at me with every bit of attention that existed within the fiber of their being.

Almost afraid to ask, with a child-like innocence, Slim cautiously blurted out,

"And?"

I took a deep breath, hopped up on one of Gus' amp cabinets and with all the energy I had in the moment I screamed out,

"AND KICK SOME MOTHER FUCKING ASS TOMORROW!"

We all cheered and hugged like the brothers we were. But coming out of that rehearsal and as they all knew from the beginning, I had to keep my vision alive and that band would live on without them if they chose not to be a part of it and we were all okay and comfortable knowing that the festival would be the perfect bookend for that line up of the band.

After rehearsal, we packed our gear into Blake's van and made our final preparations for the festival the next day. With graduation behind us, a lot hung in the balance of that show.

If we won the trip to LA, our immediate future would be certain. I wasn't going to college in the fall so the move to LA was vital for my next steps in life regardless. Even Blake was willing to give the trip a shot as long as it didn't interfere with his college entrance in September.

I guess more would be revealed in the next few days, but the first matter was to kick ass at the festival and try to impress the judges who were offering the concessionary prizes.

4

DON'T LOOK BACK

AS I WOKE UP the next morning, the day of
the most important show of my life at that point;
I had a nervous but positive disposition. I called
Blake to make sure he had everything in order
with the gear, had printed out our set lists, and
was running on time for our 10am arrival at the
festival site.

Blake was an honest and reliable guy. I guess
that's why he played bass. He was the anchor of
our band and never caused any real problems,
and he was my go-to guy for logistics. I truly
hoped he would stick with me and the
band. Slim was going to ride with him and I was
picking up Gus at 9am to head over to the festival.

As Gus and I pulled up to the security gate,
you could see the carnival rides and feel the
sense of summertime fun all around. There was a

sense of grandness that the festival was mounting and it was the big event for Iowa that summer, and we were part of it!

The headliners buses and trucks lined the backstage area and we were quickly instructed to a small cubicle tent area next to the catering building backstage. Our backstage dressing room was nothing impressive, but it was adequate for us to place our suitcases, guitars and have a landing pad before and after the show.

Family and friends, including girlfriends, were instructed days prior to leave us alone that day until our set was over by mid-afternoon. That show was hopefully going to be our big break and any distractions had to be pushed to the side.

One concern I had was Slim cracking open any alcohol before the show. He wasn't a drunk, but he drank a few beers in the sun at an outdoor keg party show we did the previous summer and he was shitfaced before we even got onstage. He somehow fell into his own drum kit while playing it!

As impressive and hilarious as that was then, that wasn't going to fly during the show that day, and we were all under the legal drinking age, so I took precautions to keep any booze out of our dressing room area.

The show production organizers came by to give us our credentials and the run-down of the day. I asked if there was a guy named Robert DiAngelis anywhere to be found and was told he was quite busy with the festival but his right-hand man Vinny Lucata would be around later to see us.

Vinny, it seemed, was the one tasked with handling the contest portion of the event, the portion that most interested me. It seemed it was Vinny and his crew we needed to impress the most in order to win the contest, so I kept my eye out for him as the clock crept closer to our show time of 2pm.

We were escorted to the stage around 1pm as the band guys loaded our gear from the van onto the stage. Most of the larger items, like the amplifiers and drums, were already provided for us by the festival; which, from what I gathered, was common with large festival side stages like that. It's known as back lining.

All we needed to pay attention to was our guitar effects pedals and the couple of extra staging ramps the festival agreed to let us use, as long as they were loaded quickly on and off the stage prior to, and after our set.

I kept my eye out for Vinny amongst the growing crowd of people hovering around the stage, all of whom wore their laminate credentials hanging off around their necks, and all of whom kept their cool like they knew what was going on with the festival and the stage area.

A cute young professional woman named Sarah (it was printed on her credential) quickly approached as we were doing a quick sound check of our gear about 10 minutes prior to our set. She offered a quick introduction,

"I'm with The Sayer Agency in Los Angeles, and we are really looking forward to your show. I've heard a lot about you and your band so break a leg and I'll look for you after your set so we can chat more."

I was nervously impressed, not only because she was very sexy in her tight yoga pants and fitted festival shirt, but she also seemed to have a convincing manner, which indicated that we might have had the show in the bag already. I was suspicious, but her charming mannerisms spoke to my testosterone and actually got me pumped for the show even more.

I don't know how it is for most guys, but for me, I would always love having hot girls looking at me while performing. It was as if I got to go into character and pretend I was an actor, maybe even a porn star actually. It would be those moments onstage where I'd feel like I owned the world and hot girls who might not give me the time of day offstage, were suddenly my concubine slaves when I'd be onstage.

There's a great album cover by Kiss called "Love Gun" and the girls are ogling over the four band members standing before them. That was a pretty good description of how I felt whenever I'd be onstage; like an adorned god with my goddesses at my beckon call.

At 1:58 pm, the four of us band members huddled behind the drum kit for a quick rally and pre-show pep talk, which always included a sort of prayer-meets-battle cry to get us pumped up for the show. As we concluded, a cute but bitchy little blonde woman named Becky, who was in charge of the stage, gave the cue for us to take the stage and start our show.

At exactly 2pm, I entered the stage from the right and looked toward Slim as he clicked his sticks four times for us to begin a ringing E chord for the rest of the band to enter stage. I took the microphone center stage and announced,

"Hello Rock Fest, we are Villain! We have come here to chew bubblegum and kick ass, but guess what? We're all out of bubblegum, mother fuckers!"

I began the intro riff to our show opening song "Hard, Fast & Loud", one of our most up-tempo and thrashing songs which always got the crowd excited, even if they didn't know us or the song. It had a similar feel to Motley Crue's "Kickstart My Heart" and got everyone on their feet, even the people half way back who initially seemed content to sit on their beach towels for the early afternoon.

As we rocked our way through the set, it seemed the rock gods were on our side and the show went off without a hitch. The sound was decent and there was a clear chemistry to our performance.

At exactly 2:30pm, right on schedule, we hit our final chord, took a bow and I said our final,

"Goodbye Rock Fest! We've been Villain, and you've been fucking great! I hope we kicked your ass, because you sure kicked ours! We'll see you again soon!"

Sweaty from our performance, we made our way off the stage to the dressing room area as our two friends acting as roadies cleared the stage of our personal gear. But, not before Sarah, from The Sayer Agency, caught up to me, handed me her card and enthusiastically said,

"You were amazing, and I mean YOU! Take a few minutes to relax and I'll be back to see you in your dressing room. We need to talk."

I was taken aback. The band kicked ass and I was pretty sure we'd be a hard act to follow for any other contestants at the festival, but Sarah seemed extremely focused on me. I was going to follow her lead.

Suddenly, my mind swirled; was it the band they wanted, or just me? What would I say to the other guys if they singled me out and they were left behind? They knew that Villain was my baby but I at least wanted them to have the opportunity to drive forward with me even though I knew they had alternate plans with their lives.

As much as I always knew my destiny was on the stages of rock n roll, I also liked to have my team around me. Sarah's comment got me thinking about scenarios that might separate the men from the boys, and as much as I hated to admit it right then and there, I was ready for it.

As we toweled off in our dressing room tent, I kept my cool and gushed congratulations on the guys for a kick ass show. I hoped they didn't see Sarah singling me out after our set. It was an awkward moment but I was also anxious for my impending discussion with her any minute now.

I encouraged the guys to meet up with their families and girlfriends, in hopes they wouldn't see me one on one with Sarah. It would be uncomfortable for me to be hauled off with her and leave the other guys behind and anything I could do to avoid that awkward moment was fine by me.

As the family members came back to give their congratulations on our performance, the band guys seemed intent on watching the other acts on the bill and getting in some fun carnival time with their friends; which left me alone in the dressing room for a stretch just convenient enough for Sarah to stop in and invite me over to her production office nearby. It seemed, she too, was waiting for a quiet moment to stop by to catch me without distraction of the other band members.

In the back of my mind I was hoping it would either unfold with a record contract or as a porno. Would it have been too much to ask for both?

With an almost flirtatious hitherto, she softly stroked my back with her right hand, whisked me into her office, and offered me a drink. I told her water would be fine and she indicated to me to have a chair to sit down for a chat.

Quickly, she sat her small and perfect frame down across from me at a little round table and held my hand in her small but firm grip as she began her spiel of how she is a field rep for a large and respected firm called The Sayer Agency, with offices in Los Angeles, New York, London, Tokyo, Dubai, Sao Paulo, Moscow, Tel Aviv and Hong Kong.

She explained that their agency was a complete talent agency, but so much more, they covered bookings for musicians, actors and authors, artist management, legal matters and even represented certain political figures.

Her pitch was educated and slick; plus, her slight sexual innuendos only helped her to connect to my synapsis, which were still firing like an orgasm from our show, just 30 minutes prior.

There was something about a hot looking woman giving you her attention after a show; It was like the same adrenaline I would feel on that stage. I guess that was why so many musicians liked drugs and sex backstage, as a way to recreate that rush we would get from the audience on stage.

Sarah continued that while they at Sayer retained the biggest and most respected talent across the entertainment industry, they also utilized regional and local festivals like that one to mine for new and upcoming talent.

She explained that although many established entertainers reside in major cities, the fresh new talent often reside in unsuspecting places of the Midwest and interior regions of any given country.

Her sparkly green eyes were mesmerizing as she described the global reach of The Sayer Agency. I found myself undressing her in my mind, which led to wild sexual fantasies of us engaged in a sensation of wild rock star anecdotes.

I somehow had a feeling she had taken part in all that before and I was just an amateur she could cast her spell on. Well, she had me; hook line and sinker. It was as if she wielded a spell over me and I was hers. She was convincing but most of all, I was in. Whatever she wanted; I was there for the taking.

She told me of a great new band in Hollywood which The Sayer Agency was grooming to become their next big act. They had four major record labels at the door ready to tender their offers for a recording contract to the band.

She went on to explain that what she saw in me was real rock star charisma, something on the super star level of Jon Bon Jovi. Not just a rock star, but a super star.

She explained there would be coaching and extensive grooming necessary to get me to the top, but fundamentally I had the goods along with real raw natural talent and the gusto to back it up.

I took a few days after the festival to process what had just transpired. I had essentially been offered the break of a lifetime, but it meant moving on from Villain. These guys were my friends, and we tried hard to move the needle of fame in that area, but no doubt it was going to be a tough uphill battle.

At the end of the day, the offer was made to me, not Villain. Plus, high school was over and Blake had his plans for college in the fall anyway; so, in a way, Villain was at a crossroads re-gardless. I had to tell the guys I was moving to California without them.

I scheduled a meeting the next day to break the news to the band. As much as there was some initial grumbling and disappointment, in a way they sort of understood and knew that my ambi-tions were always bigger than theirs. It was time to move on and they gave me their blessing.

I called Sarah to accept her offer and the plans were set in motion. They secured me an apartment in Hollywood where I would stay at in few weeks once I arrived. I broke the news to my parents and they were cautiously optimistic about the whole thing. Parents being parents, and all.

Two weeks later I cleared out my bank ac-count of $2400 and packed all my gear into the back of my Ford F-150 pickup truck with a camper top to protect my equipment and suitcase of clothes. I pulled onto the highway out of Delane and never looked back.

New horizons lay ahead.

I was fucking doing it.

5

WE'RE NOT IN KANSAS ANYMORE

PULLING INTO HOLLYWOOD WAS a certain culture shock. It was funny; it looked nothing like all the TV shows I grew up watching with beautiful girls in bikinis, fancy cars and clear blue skies. In reality, it was an overcrowded, polluted, run-down dump of a city.

The roads were terrible in my Ford truck and I was sure my guitars and amps were taking a beating in the back with all the potholes. Even the palm trees were gasping for breath as the smog robbed them of their valiant effort to grace the once clear blue skies of that supposedly, once-most beautiful state in our union. Maybe in years past it was nice, but certainly not the day I pulled into that god-forsaken hellhole.

Sarah and The Sayer Agency paid rent for me in a decent little studio apartment just off Hollywood Blvd so I at least have a place to land. The lease was paid free and clear for six months so it was a start.

Apparently, The Sayer Agency were pretty certain I'd have a gig by then and things would proceed to get rolling financially as well. I had no choice but to trust them and the 12-month contract I signed with them before departing Delane the week prior.

I didn't know how they rolled in Hollywood but I had enough personal funds with me to get a small part time job to pay the rent and eat just in case everything fell apart.

From what Sarah assured me, I'd be fine as long as I followed instructions from Mr. Sayer himself along with his team of knowledgeable and seasoned professionals.

As I pulled up to my apartment on Orange Ave, located smack dab between Hollywood and Sunset Boulevards, and directly across the street from Hollywood High School, I surveyed the neighborhood and began to appreciate my small-town upbringing.

Hollywood High looked more like a prison than a high school. I couldn't figure out if the barbed wire fence was to keep the students in, or keep the thugs out. Probably a bit of both, I figured.

I called Sarah to let her know I had arrived and was heading to the apartment manager's office to get my keys. She assured me everything was in order and all I'd have to do is sign a couple of lease documents to get my keys and I'd be set. She was right. I met the manager, signed the docs to get my keys and I began to unload my gear into the furnished apartment.

Settling in, I set up my amps in my modest little apartment living room and plugged in to warm up on some chords and solo pieces. It was about 10am and immediately I heard a loud banging on the wall and yelling from what would be my next-door neighbor,

"Shut the fuck up asshole! You're not the only one who lives here, ya know?!"

Was that Hollywood's welcome greeting to me?

Turning down my amps a bit, I continued shredding some licks but the banging and screaming from next door continued. I put my guitar down and walked next door to try and make peace with my neighbor. As I knocked on the door, I heard,

"What the fuck do you want, I'm trying to sleep?"

Puzzled, I said, "Sorry about the noise, I just got into town, I'll keep it down."

Nothing in reply.

Going back to my apartment, I threw a pinch of my Iowa ditch weed marijuana into my bong and took a quick hit to get my head straight before heading up to the convenience store on Hollywood Blvd to grab some munchies.

As I left, I noticed the angry next-door neighbor's door was open, and like a shadow, out walked a clearly visible rock star type guy wearing sunglasses and his hair up under a baseball cap. Presumably, he was the one I agitated earlier in the morning with my guitar playing being too loud.

Offering a kind Midwest opening introduction, I said a quick hello and gave a subtle apology. That was how we would do it in Delane. Hell, we left our keys in the car at night, left doors unlocked to our homes and when neighbors stop by unannounced, we invited them in for coffee and a hang.

Judging by the pulse of LA these past several hours, I wasn't so sure that was the code in Hollywood. People seemed driven, kept mostly to themselves and garnered a tight sphere around them in a way that clearly said, *leave me the fuck alone*.

Slowly, and through a visible late-night hangover, my neighbor grumbled,

"You the one playing guitar this morning?"

"Yeah, that was me. Sorry about the early wake up call, I just got into town yesterday and was just getting settled in."

He seemed unaffected. Trying to diffuse the offense a bit more, I held out my hand for a handshake or fist bump, and offered my name,

"Hey, I'm Sledge."

He said,

"I'm Robin. Aren't you the guy Sarah said would be coming by this week?"

"Yeah that's me! She said to get settled in and I would be making some introductions to a group she's managing out here".

Robin replied,

"Yeah, cool. Let's meet up later after I get some grub and regroup from last night. This town's crazy, ya know!"

I nodded assuredly, left it at that, and got on my way.

As I headed out of the apartment building, I began to people watch and take in my surroundings. Hollywood Blvd. was filled with tourists; probably from the likes of Iowa, who looked like they had no clue where they were, nor any sense of street hustle.

Aside from the tourists, the streets were loaded with panhandlers, drug hustlers and a few girls in high heels and short skirts, who were either up past their bedtime, or getting their game on for the night ahead; clearly prostitutes.

I also noticed quite a few musicians in the area, probably because of a well-known guitar vocational school a couple blocks to the east. I'd seen ads for the school in guitar publications back in Delane and often thought about enrolling there; but to me, higher education had no place in rock n roll.

I knew it was all about selling charisma as much as your chops and it was also a young man's game, so why exhaust precious time when time was on my side? I was there to hit the ground runnin' with a band and with Sarah footin' the bill, there would always be time for school.

One thought which kept coming back to me was that Robin clearly held himself with an air of rock stardom, a charm I noticed most of the wanna-be's on Hollywood Blvd were lacking.

Sure, they looked like rock stars, but you could tell it wasn't in their blood. Something about my quick interaction with Robin told me a different story. He seemed to beat to a different drum and seemed unaffected by the mundane things like waking up to go to work or any sort of integration into the society around him.

In other words, he was rock n roll incarnate. My work ethic was different, maybe because I wasn't jaded by Hollywood yet; still, my gut told me something was off about Robin, but I'd play along and see how things went.

I set my sights on trying to connect with him again; either by chance in the hallway, or an intentional knock on his door that week. Maybe a peace offering consisting of a 12 pack of beer and a few buds would do the trick. It was a Tuesday so I set my sights on that Friday as our day of destiny.

As luck would have it, when I got back to the apartment a couple of hours later, Robin was at his door; that time with a stunningly good looking, long legged female who looked like she was ready for anything rock n roll. I wouldn't say she was Penthouse Magazine material, but certainly Hustler Magazine would cut it.

I was impressed and my instincts seemed right about Robin. He was the real deal. He looked over as I approached my front door, about ten feet away, and said,

"Hey, it's the new guy in town."

His girl gave me a sort of apologetic smile on his behalf, which quickly got my attention.

Threesome perhaps?

Probably not, but certainly she had friends I could meet. I smiled and quickly reframed a more, 'I'm getting the town figured out already' sort of response, which was clearly bullshit. It sounded a little something like this,

"Hot today, isn't it?"

As the words came out of my mouth, I felt like a fool. Clearly, no one assimilated into that neighborhood that quickly; it was the first point of entry for newbies like me, and Robin and his girl knew it.

Looking at the brown bag full of beer under my arm, Robin quickly and playfully asked,

"Whatcha got there, newbie? Wanna come over and share some of your morning juice with us all? It's not nice to bogart beer so early in the day."

Yep, he was shaking a hangover all right and it seemed as though I had the magical elixir to set the mood straight. I replied,

"Yeah, good call, let me grab something inside and I'll be right over. Give me two minutes."

Even though he was kind of a standoffish dick, it was my chance to finally make a few friends.

I ran over to my apartment, grabbed some of my weed, a small pipe, and made my way over to Robin's. He quickly introduced me to his girl Mercedes. Women didn't have names like that back in Delane, instead using more Christian names like Julie, Stephanie, Teresa, etc.

Mercedes was a sophisticated name, which spoke to the more international pool of hipsters I would be hanging with in a multi-cultural city like LA.

She had a nice dark complexion, likely Italian or even Hispanic, and she smelled good with her sweet oily perfume. She had a short fur coat and even shorter skirt to reveal her long slinky legs. Clearly, she had rock n roll style, and I liked it!

Robin put some vinyl on the turntable and began to crank up the volume. Okay, so that was when we were able to be loud there, which was whenever Robin felt like it.

A slight smell of patchouli oil hung in the background, so I offered up my 12 pack of beer and some of my pot. As the beers opened and the aroma of weed began to circulate around the apartment, Robin began telling a story, his history and rock n' roll background.

He had grown up in California and had obvious street smarts. It seemed that while he had rock n' roll charm, he could be a sort of snake charmer, too. Apparently, rock n' roll just happened to be where he could sell his bullshit, and wasn't necessarily a passion for him. It was the avenue life handed him, where he could hold his own amongst the swindlers and con men in the music industry.

As his story unfolded, apparently, he was part of a band that was getting some major traction on the Sunset Strip. Record labels were looming and he seemed confidant a deal was imminent. It sounded a lot like the band Sarah was promising for me to join, so I inquired.

Robin confirmed that, yes, there was a third-party talent agency in Beverly Hills who had recently stepped in to help broker the negotiations between the band and record companies, courting his band to be signed to a very lucrative multi-album deal.

While Robin took a hit off my pipe, he explained that there was an inevitable lineup change coming before the deal would be inked; but he seemed dismissive of any disruption that might cause him. He went on to brag,

"I'm the singer of the band and you can't replace the voice of a group so I know my job is secure."

Mercedes snuggled up to him on the couch in a manner that exuded confidence that she would be along for the ride with Robin. Noticeably, he offered little affection to her as his stories flowed; all the while the beer and weed continued to ease his hangover.

It was at that point I let him know how Sarah had discovered me with my band at the Iowa Rock Fest; that she felt confident I would be the right fit for a band getting ready to be signed to a major record deal and that it seemed Robin's band might be that band. Setting down his beer, Robin looked me squarely in the eye and said,

"Well Sledge, here's how it goes; I've been busting my ass getting this band off the ground for two years now. I've got a bit of a reputation where folks say I drink a bit too much and fight even more."

"But the truth is I AM this band, son. I've got a kick ass drummer, lead guitarist and bass player behind me, and they write some great songs, but they aren't shit without me. So, I hope you play guitar or something, because we sure as shit don't need another singer around here."

Robin made his point loud and clear. He was the alpha dog and rightfully so. I understood where he was coming from with building his band up from the ground up and at that point in time, he was finally the big fish in a big pond.

I got a sense that Mercedes was sizing me up, not so much in a flirtatious way, but more so as match maker. Clearly, if there were more women like her where she came from, I got the sense that she would be more comfortable if I had a woman next me instead of her being the only female in the room.

I also sensed that she was playing queen bee next to her man in order to maintain her position at the top of the food chain; she would be the one bringing the other ladies around. I was the new guy, so I played along. Plus, I'd like to be hanging more with the echelon of women like Mercedes so I was up to see how she played the game.

Quickly, she offered,

"Hey, you know what? I should call Brittany so we can head down to The Masquerade Bar later for some drinks and dinner."

BINGO!

I was in!

I had no idea what Brittany looked like, and I didn't care. I had broken things off with my girl, Jessica, back home in Delane before the summer as I knew I couldn't have a girl waiting for me back home once things were heating up for Villain at the Iowa Rock Fest.

I was on a mission of global domination for my career and a woman backhome would only cloud my emotions and distract my focus. So, to have some companionship for that night, and maybe even get laid in my first week in LA, was all-good by me.

Mercedes whipped up the plan and we were set. I went next door to my apartment to freshen up and by 9pm we were headed out the door to the infamous Masquerade Bar on Sunset Blvd, next to The Foxy Theater.

As it turned out, The Masquerade Bar was a place every legendary and hoped-to-be rock star hung out. As we pulled in, there was a line out the door with two bullish doormen the size of refrigerators making the decision who got in and who didn't.

As we walked up, the doormen greeted Robin and Mercedes with hugs and kisses and we were quickly whisked inside to a booth toward the back of the restaurant.

The other booths and tables lining the walls and main floor area were filled with rocker looking guys and gals. Some of them looked familiar, famous yet clearly in disguise in what was a darkened den of iniquity.

It seemed it was the place where the music industry connected, and for anyone hoping to hook-up via the nightlife on the strip. It was like there was a secret code everyone knew and no one gave off any air of fan-boy. So, for me, I played it cool and acted like I belonged there.

I saw a couple of my rock n' roll heroes nestled up to their ladies in a couple of the more discreet booths, women who shared a similar flare for rock n' roll like Mercedes.

Once seated, the waitress took our drink and food order and exchanged friendly cheek to cheek kisses to Robin and Mercedes. Clearly, they were regulars there and I observed their mannerisms so I would know to do the same once I got accepted into that particular elite club of rock n' roller musicians.

After a few minutes, a foxy yet slightly different but equally as sexy version of Mercedes slipped into our booth next to me. She was introduced as Brittany and suddenly I perked up. She was pretty with a cuteness about her that felt a bit more relaxed than Mercedes' demeanor.

Within minutes of our conversation, I got to know that she was a Denver, Colorado girl who had come to Hollywood seeking ambitions of being a TV or film star. But, for the time being, she danced at one of the full nude bars on La Cienega called The Strip.

She said she had an agent and went on to list off a handful of bit parts she starred in, none of which seemed significant. I got the feeling that she was slugging it out with the hope that if she landed a co-starring role for a television pilot or something like that, she would finally be taken seriously.

I listened and nodded along to her chatty resume and 'who's who' she claimed to know around town, but as her fancy perfume wafed my way, I was more interested in getting lucky with her than spending too much time with the small talk. The feeling seemed mutual.

Quickly, she was out of our booth and hob knobbing the restaurant; exchanging the same phony cheek to cheek kisses as our waitress exchanged with Robin and Mercedes.

Clearly, Brittany was a "girl about town" and it seemed the other rockers in the room knew of her. I took the cue to not get too close to be assumed a fool, but close enough to make my play with her.

By the time our food came, Brittany was back and quickly escorted me out of my seat saying,

"I want to introduce you to Brett, he's the singer of this great new band who just landed a record deal."

As she towed me up the stairs past the bar, we found a small lounge off to the side with soft chill music playing. She quickly settled me into her arms on the large opium-den type pillows, which were layered around the seating area. Conveniently, the little pillow area had curtains situated in a way that indicated illicit drug use and even sex would be the norm here.

It was the perfect time to strike a kiss on her big ruby lips, which she received with no hesitation. As my hands made their way down her waist, onto her thin silky stockings, she reached down onto my crotch, where I was growing one hell of a hard on.

Looking like Hollywood was my kinda town! Back in Delane, it would take several dinners and movie dates to get as far as I had gotten with Brittany in just under an hour.

Suddenly, my hand was up her skirt and inside her as I felt her hips pulsate, driving my hand deeper. With porno like groans in my ear, she whispered,

"Come here and let me fuck you."

With the ease of a pro, she had my pants unzipped and my throbbing man-piece out as she landed herself on top of me with me deep inside her. As my hands grabbed around behind her ass, she was already grinding on top of me.

For a quick moment, I realized we were in a public bar with other patrons nearby, but that thought was fleeting and we carried on.

Having not been laid for a few weeks, I exploded inside her and she went limp on top of me as we lay back on the pillows to recharge.

Without missing a beat, she had her stockings up around her waist, and reset herself to hit the bar as if nothing had happened.

Swiftly, she grabbed my hand and pulled me back downstairs to settle in again with Robin and Mercedes. We never did meet Brett, not that I minded, and as we approached the booth, Mercedes met my eyes with a wink that deserved a quick thumbs up from me. I owed her one after that. She had that town wired, and knew the girls who were players. God bless her and all of Hollywood.

I tried to keep up drinking with Robin, but the guy was a pro. At one point, he had six shots of tequila lined up and was ready to plow right through them. I gave him a look of concern and blurted out,

"Dude, are you going to be okay after that?!"

He slyly looked over at me and said,

"Why? Are you gonna hold my hair if I get sick?"

We all shared a good laugh from that exchange. But with all the knowledge and lifestyle tips I had been learning from Robin, you damn well better believe I'd be there to hold his hair if it ever got to that point.

Robin and I connected that evening; not just as musicians but as friends. I made sure to keep my emotional distance from getting too attached, though. I genuinely liked the dude but I had to take all of his advice under consideration and not get too close to anybody out there. I couldn't be too trusting; especially in a place like Hollywood. As long as I prepared for the worst but hope for the best, I figured I would be fine.

As the night wore on and the drinks and food flowed, I came to realize the trick there was to play the game, but falling in love or getting committed were not part of the rules. In fact, they would only set you back while someone else swooped in to take your place.

As the booze buzz set in, my mind drifted
back to Delane, and all I could think was,
"You're not in Kansas anymore."

6

ALL SIN, NO VIRGIN

A FEW DAYS AFTER The Masquerade Bar, which left me sexually satisfied and professionally feeling like I was becoming a part of the fabric of Hollywood, my next step was to get in the room with Robin and start getting connected to him musically.

It was only through a bizarre meeting of fate that I learned he was the guy whom The Sayer Agency was connecting me with anyhow; I was just a little ahead of them.

His band Virgin Sinner were reportedly the next big thing to break around town and with The Sayer Agency at the helm, along with a lucrative record deal on the table, the future looked bright.

It seemed that The Sayer Agency knew what they were doing and acted as a good matchmaker when finding the right talent to groom for stardom. I was a bit hesitant that it might be some kind of heavy metal boy band, but it looked to be the real deal and I was the next in line. My aim was to shut my mouth, pay attention and enjoy the ride. The only loose cannon seemed to be Robin.

I spent a lot of time with Robin during those first two weeks. He had a hard-assed mentor sort of vibe about him like a rock n' roll Mr. Miyagi and I listened to every word he said. He was a visionary, like myself, and I believe we both connected over that.

Through our many talks, I think we both let our guards down and really understood each other. Even though we were from different worlds, we were able to find common ground and a solid friendship. He even began leaving his door unlocked for me; mainly because my constant knocking would just piss him off.

There was one instance with Robin that did hit me the wrong way though, which would eventually help paint a better picture of who he actually was.

One evening, I was bored in my apartment and was almost tone deaf from practicing guitar so much that I ran down to the grocery store and picked up a case of beer for Robin and I to plow through. It was going to be one of *those* kinds of nights. I knew he was home because I could hear him knocking around in his apartment like he always did.

As I was walking through the complex hallway with the soon to be obliterated case of beer under my arm, I had an uneasy feeling wash over me. I didn't know what it was or how I should have felt but my gut was definitely trying to tell me something. I cracked open a can of beer to shut my gut up so I could get on with our eventual mini bender of an evening.

I crept into his apartment like I usually did. One of my favorite hobbies during that time was silently entering Robin's apartment with ninja like precision and scaring the shit out of him. His reactions were always priceless even though he would end up punching me in the arm with full force afterwards; it was totally worth it!

As I entered the apartment, I already noticed something was off. I smelled something funny; it almost smelled like chemicals; not quite cleaning materials and not quite gasoline. It was very strange.

I silently stalked my way into his kitchen. He was nowhere in sight, but that odd-smell became more pungent. I then noticed the bathroom door was closed so I put two and two together and figured he ate something completely fucked up and was just taking a monumental shit. Hence the weird smell.

Figuring that was the case, I sat in front of the bathroom door with the case of beer and waited to give Robin what would surely be the scare of his life. I silently began cracking open beers to help pass the time; I knew that it would be worth the wait. I remember thinking,

What kind of frightened face would he make this time?

After about 20 minutes and 6 beers into our 24 pack, I began to get a bit buzzed. Although I didn't hear anything happening in the bathroom, I kept waiting.

Then after 45 minutes and well halfway through the case of beer, I had had enough and began knocking on the bathroom door.

Nothing.

I began pounding harder and harder and yelled,

"Robin! It's Sledge! What the fuck are you doing in there?!"

Not a peep.

I tried the doorknob but it was locked so I tried to shoulder-open the door and nothing.

Shit.

Did he OD? I mean I knew he dabbled in drugs but my brain couldn't help but think about all the dead rock star stories of lore. If he was trying to pay me back by scaring me then he definitely had the upper hand. Either way, I ran into

THE SLEDGE CHRONICLES: ROCK STAR HITMAN

his kitchen and found a bobby pin and a few other small items so I could pick the lock. A little talent I gained out of boredom from growing up in Delane.

After a few moments I got the lock and opened the door. To say I was in complete disgusted shock would be an understatement. I didn't know whether to laugh, cry, or call an ambulance.

Apart from that awful smell completely hitting me in the face from its source, that being a burnt spoon with some kind of drug cooked onto it, on the toilet was Robin, as expected, but he was passed out leaning back and had a needle sticking out of his arm.

He would never show off his arms, which always made me curious, and at that moment I knew why. They were covered in so many sores and scars that he looked like a fresh burn victim. His pants were around his ankles and in front of him was a random girl I had never seen before, also covered in sores and passed out in Robin's lap with his limp dick in her mouth. I was filled with so many questions,

What was I looking at?

Was this normal?

What the fuck do I do?

I began to shake Robin to wake up. The girl lazily fell sideways and hit her head against the bathroom wall jolting her awake to groggily and angrily say,

"What the fuck, man?"

After a moment, she quickly found comfort on the tile floor and passed back out. I drew my attention back to Robin and yelled,

"Robin! Wake the fuck up dude! Are you okay?!"

I shook him more and more,

"Robin! What the fuck, man?!"

He then began to softly laugh; a reaction I was not expecting. He slowly lifted up his head and somehow was able to look me in the eyes even though his eyes were shut. He continued to laugh harder and harder. Then the girl on the floor began to laugh as well. I didn't know if I should laugh as well or if I should get the hell out of there because maybe they were both possessed by some kind of Hollywood Demon.

The laughing became more hysterical and I couldn't help but make myself feel at ease with the situation at that point; even though the girl was covered in cum and Robin had his pants around his ankles. Through the maniacal laughter Robin was able to mutter out some words,

"Are you here to hold my hair, Sledge?"

This inkling of coherency on behalf of Robin made me feel at least a little bit better and I was finally able to laugh as well. I nervously blurted out,

"I guess I'm a little late to the hair holding party! But it looks like you were holding her hair pretty good!"

We then all completely lost it with laughter. I couldn't even comprehend how awful and strange that moment was. All I could do was roll with it and play along. Either this was an incredibly fucked up situation and I needed to get my friend some help immediately, or this was just how Hollywood rolls. I guess I would have to stick with the latter in that regard.

As Robin pulled his pants up and began cleaning himself up a little, he mumbled,

"So did you bring beer?"

I handed him a can and he cracked it open and chugged it. He then motioned for me to give him another one and he chugged that one as well.

I pointed to the girl and asked what to do with her and he just smiled and said,

"She's a big girl, she can take care of herself. Let's go chill on the couch."

We sat down on the couch with the remaining case of beer between us and just shared a comfortable silence with each other. I then finally asked,

"So, what the hell was that all about? Seriously."

He looked at me with a glazed over stare and without missing a beat and with a straight face said,

"That, my friend, was just a normal Tuesday. You should see what happens Wednesdays."

I let out a nervous laugh and he chuckled as well. It became apparent that no matter how close I felt to the guy, he was always going to be too far gone for me to completely care about him. Robin then laid down some knowledge on me,

"Let me tell you something, Sledge. Life in Hollywood ain't for the weak at heart."

Those words stuck with me. No matter how much I thought I knew about everything, there was always something else out there for me to grasp onto mentally.

We sat on his couch and finished our case of beer. The girl eventually came to and stumbled out of the bathroom all dolled up as if nothing happened. As she was leaving, she looked at Robin and said,

"Alright honey, thanks for a good time as always. See you next Tuesday."

Robin nodded and waved. He then turned to me and said,

"See? Tuesdays."

One thing was for sure; the guy definitely did not live up to his band's namesake; Virgin Sinner.

7

BECOMING THE DREAM

A FEW DAYS AFTER my awkward situation with Robin, Sarah had given me five of the 12 songs Virgin Sinner were preparing to record for their debut album. These would be my initial audition songs, and assuming things went well, I would be learning the remaining songs for the recording session.

My first rehearsal was scheduled two weeks after I arrived into Hollywood, at a well-known sound stage on Sunset, Blvd. I was chauffeured to the facility to make sure I arrived by 12pm.

The office manager directed me to the big sound stage toward the back of the facility and made quick introductions to a couple of the point people working inside the room.

The large stage was crowded with amplifiers, drums, microphones and road cases lining the perimeter walls. There were at least a dozen men and women diligently tending to their posts of audio, video, pyro, and recording positions.

The best I could tell, my audition was going to be filmed and recorded for the team to review. A technician named Andy approached me with a warm smile and greeting. He informed me that he was the session manager and if I needed anything, he was there for me.

Andy instructed me where I should setup on the stage. I was a bit intimidated as I stepped onto the large rehearsal platform. I played it cool and plugged my guitar into the stage left half stack amplifier, next to the drum set, where I began to tune up. I proceeded to prepare my effects pedals and adjust the height of the vocal microphone in front of me.

I was instructed by Sarah to learn the rhythm guitar parts as well as the lead vocal parts for all the songs. I found it a bit odd to have to learn the lead vocal lines, as it seemed Robin would handle those. Ironically, Robin was not in sight that day as the other three band members welcomed me on the stage with smiles and fist bumps.

As the band got busy with the rest of their equipment preparations, I asked if Robin would be along shortly to join us. I also mentioned that he and I had met at the apartment complex we were staying at which was nearby and that we were getting to know each other the past few weeks.

Sheepishly, the band members looked down at the ground and the guitar player Jimmy replied,

"Yeah, well here's the thing. Robin's not coming because this is an audition to replace him. He's not really working out. He has been taking his boozing and chemical abuse more seriously than the band. We've had three other guys in here this week, but everyone seems confident that you're gonna nail this. So let's do this, Okay?"

No wonder Sarah was so hot on getting me out there. This was a strategic plan to replace Robin before they signed the record deal. I had heard of that sort of thing happening in the business, from Robin nonetheless, but I never in a million years thought it would be me replacing someone just before their big break!

I couldn't help but feel bad but as with what Robin was teaching me, that's how the chips fall sometimes. I'd be lying if I said I didn't feel conflicted at that moment.

The drummer, Steven, counted off the first song and right away I could feel the power resonate around me. These guys were tight and meant business. I stepped up to the microphone and delivered the opening lines to a fantastic song called "Take it Or Leave It". It was a hard-hitting, but melodic song with a big hooky guitar riff. When the chorus hit, I sang it with all my heart,

"This is it, take it or leave it, no way back, no turning back."

I was taken aback by the eeriness of how the lyrics matched my situation.

You could feel the excitement in the room. I quickly felt the good vibe from the band as well. It seemed to be gelling quickly as the team in the room stopped to join in on the excitement. After the first song, everyone on the team were clapping, whistling and cheering.

We quickly moved through the remaining four songs with the same enthusiasm from the band and team.

Once we finished, we were sweaty, smiling and high fiving each other. I put my guitar down, swigged some bottled water while the drummer signaled for us all to head down off the stage and rally out by the soundboard to have a chat.

While Andy was the session boss, Steven seemed to be the one running the band and was what seemed second in command after Robin. He informed me,

"You knocked it out of the park, man! Really, great stuff. We filmed and recorded everything and will keep you posted on the next steps. We have rehearsals all next week. Not sure how much you know, but we have Panoramic Records coming down to watch the full run through of our live show."

"They have a large deal on the table for us but they need to see the band live with the new singer, which looks to be you. I think we all feel confident you're the new man for the job and we need you to be ready. We have five more rehearsals and then the final audition for Panoramic. Can you handle it?"

Stoked, somewhat intimidated and confidently, I said,

"Hell yeah I'm ready. Let's do this!"

The odd thing was, I didn't even feel like it mattered; they had made up their mind and I was in.

I began to wonder if it was fate, or if somebody had eyes on me these past few months to set the whole thing up. I didn't want to tempt fate because this was what I'd been dreaming of since I first started playing guitar. Still, it all seemed too convenient and too good to be true. I guess the next few weeks would tell me more. It was time to buckle up for what felt like the ride of a lifetime.

The following rehearsals ended up going better than ever and during my down time I found myself hanging out at a nearby convenience store in walking distance of my apartment where I would grab all my on the fly groceries, if you will.

My main draw there was this older gentleman who worked behind the counter. His name was Phil and had to have been in his mid to late sixties. He had seen Hollywood go through so many changes over the years and was so knowledgeable with the local pop-culture, which ultimately became universal pop-culture.

After my first few times in and out of the store, Phil always greeted me with a youthful enthusiasm. As if he wanted nothing more than to vicariously live through my exploits. He was always interested in hearing my stories and in return he was always able to lay down some great advice and knowledge, as the old timers usually did.

Phil eventually kind of became my adopted father figure in Hollywood. I even let him start calling me by my birth name. I was that comfortable with him. He kept me grounded.

Phil had been following my story since I had gotten to L.A. but with being so busy from rehearsals that week, I realized that I hadn't even gotten a chance to stop in and tell him that I got the gig in Virgin Sinner.

As I entered the store, I could tell Phil noticed something different about me. He said,

"Toby! Where have you been?! What happened? Did you get laid again? If you did you know you have to tell me all about it!"

His innocent and old school forward remark made me chuckle as they always did. He continued,

"Oh, come on, Toby! You and I both know the girls out here are freaky! Just don't get too freaky so you don't end up with a freaky ass love child!"

I was once again caught off guard by Phil's great sense of humor. I took a moment to compose myself.

I then said,

"I didn't quite get laid, Phil. Something better happened, believe it or not."

He replied with,

"I pretty much hit the assumption ceiling whenever good news supersedes getting laid! I'm all ears, buddy. What happened?"

I playfully paused and said,

"Well."

Phil, growing anxious shot back with,

"Well what?"

I gave the moment a few beats for drama and then laid it on him,

"I got the gig! We've been rehearsing all week which is why I haven't had a chance to stop in and tell you!"

Phil threw his hands up in the air and gave me a big hug.

"That is so wonderful, Toby!"

It felt good and meant a lot knowing someone was genuinely happy for me and my situation other than myself.

"You're living proof that hard work truly does pay off, young man! You should be so proud of yourself!"

As if my glow couldn't shine any more, it did. Phil, went on to say,

"So your career is finally getting in motion out here! Man, I love it when people get to actually come out to this hell hole and make their dreams come true."

"Thanks so much, Phil, it truly means a lot."

Phil then went into story telling mode as he often did,

"I was so worried that you were going to end up going the route that 90% of the wannabes out here end up taking which usually ends with you being perpetually doped up and waiting for fortune to come find you in the gutter."

"I tell ya, the only way any kind of fortune comes to find you in that situation is when you're featured on some day time talk show where the host is trying to determine whether or not you're the daddy."

I chuckled but listened intently on what Phil had to say,

"There was someone out here recently for the same reasons as you, actually. I haven't seen him in a minute now that I think of it."

"I forgot his name though; it'll come to me. But anyway, he had stars in his eyes just like you. And I tell ya, if I've seen it once, I've seen it a thousand times; this town has the potential to eat you alive and the sick twist is that Hollywood is always hungry."

"So anyways, this kid had so much potential. He was talented and had the right look and attitude to pragmatically take on whatever it took to make it in this business. Then one morning he came in reeking of alcohol. "

"I started growing concerned. I really took a liking to this kid so I let him slide this one time before I said anything. Then this one time turned into 6 or 7 times."

"There's nothing wrong with partying but I noticed this was becoming a habit; a bad one. Around then is when I started noticing the track marks on his arms."

"At first he was embarrassed about it anytime I'd draw attention to it but he just said that he was donating blood to earn some extra cash while he was out here. He then began making sure he had his arms covered whenever he came in after that."

"I gave him the benefit of doubt though but every time he would come in, I could literally see the years falling off the back end of this young man's life. I finally sat him down and tried to knock some sense into him."

"I cared about the kid and I couldn't live with myself if I didn't know I at least tried to get him on the right track. Like most, he heard me but didn't hear me, if you know what I mean."

"He mentioned that he was still on track for glory and that everything would work out in his favor in the end. He said that he was just in a funk but he still had his pending record deal and once he was able to get out on the road and start touring, he would fall back into a healthy routine."

"There was still some glow left in his eyes and I truly wished him the best. As he progressively got worse, he mentioned to me that he suspected that his band and management were on track to replace him."

"I contributed this assumption to his paranoid ramblings so didn't think anything of it, after all; a contract is a contract."

"A few days after this, I caught him passed out in the bathroom with a needle in his arm. It broke my fucking heart but after I woke him up with a bucket of water, I had to ban him from the store. I looked him straight in the eyes and told him, 'You have the whole world in the palm of your hands. You have something that everyone else in the world wishes they had and you need to start taking this seriously or else just like the clouds above, it's all going to inevitably just pass you by'. He nodded and left. That was the last time I saw him."

"I truly hope he got his act together otherwise I wouldn't be surprised if he got pinched for robbin' a liquor store eventually. Wait a second. Robbin'. Rob- Robbin'- Robin! That was his name! Robin!"

I froze in silence. I couldn't help but be reminded of the fact that I had just robbed my friend's life and dreams from under him when the whole time he thought I was just going to be the new guitar player and a brother. I didn't know that he suspected that he was being replaced and was deteriorating from the inside out. He seemed so confident!

As together as I thought I was with this whole situation, hearing it from Phil just really drove it home for me. As fucked up as he was, I still cared about Robin and I couldn't help but feel guilty for him slipping into his drug induced gutter. It washed over me like an instant sickness. I asked Phil,

"When was the last time you saw him?"

"This all went down about a week ago."

I had the sudden realization that I had not seen Robin for a good while at that point. After that fateful "Tuesday" I distanced myself from him a bit but in the back of my mind, thought that he was able to keep his shit together for Virgin Sinner.

The last time I spoke to him he mentioned that he would see me at my audition which obviously he was not a part of. I had been so busy with rehearsals that I hadn't had a chance to check in on him.

I was worried and needed to find Robin.

I gave Phil another big hug and said our farewells for the day. He left me with,

"Don't just dream, kid; become the dream!"

I ran back to my apartment and dropped off my pseudo groceries so I could go hunt down Robin to make sure he was okay. Just as I was walking out the door, my phone rang. I picked it up and the voice said,

"Sledge, we need you back at rehearsal. We already have a car waiting for you outside."

I didn't recognize the voice but they were surely from The Sayer Agency.

I questioned the voice,

"But I was just at the rehearsal space?"

They replied with,

"As per our contractual agreement, you are needed when needed, sir. By the way, congratulations; we at the agency hope you're ready for what's to come."

I said,

"Thanks."

Surely, they knew I had already gotten the gig with Virgin Sinner a week prior so why would they congratulate me?

I had to put off my search for Robin for the time being. I never felt so bittersweet before in my life but thinking about it in that moment; with the talks I had with him, he seemed like the type of guy to pick himself back up quickly.

Robin seemed strong willed and determined and knew the business well. I was sure he was going to be fine. The butterflies in my stomach soon fluttered away any ill-will I had toward myself once the comforting thought of the fact that I was 'making it' washed over me.

Worse comes to worse, I'd help Robin pay for rehab to get himself straight. Shit, I knew I was going to be able to afford it. I'd even help him put a new band together too.

Everything was going to be all right.

Right?

8

WAS IT ALL WORTH IT?

THE IMPROMPTU REHEARSAL END-ED up kicking off very awkwardly after I had brought up my concern about Robin. The band seemed to have had written him off as a human being. They put stories into my head about how he had begun stealing equipment from the rehearsal spot to pawn for drugs to keep up with his habit.

It felt so strange hearing this; especially with how much I thought I had gotten to know Robin and understood his eccentricities. Aside from being a little rough around the edges personality wise, he seemed to have had his faculties in order.

It was so weird, but I guess you really never do know someone, especially in Hollywood. Being from such a small Midwestern town, I never dealt with that kind of drug culture; weed was about it. I attributed the situation to my learning curve of the world of Hollywood.

Aside from all that, rehearsal went brilliantly. We plowed through the set five times and it sounded amazing. I really felt like I was putting my personal stamp on the material and we were no doubt getting tighter as a unit. We were all eagerly awaiting recording our album. We knew it was going to be beyond killer.

At the end of rehearsal, as I was leaving, Sarah ran out to catch me before I had gotten into the vehicle.

She said,

"Sledge! Come back in, we have something you need to see."

I followed Sarah back in and the rehearsal spot was pitch black as if within the few moments it took me to get to the car, everything had been shut down and everyone had gone home. Needless to say, I was pretty confused.

Then from the dark abyss, I saw a flash and then a pop. In that split second, I thought I was a goner. The lights returned and everyone had party hats on, and proceeded to yell,

"Surprise! We did it!"

Even Phil was there! I was so befuddled.

Everyone cheered, shot silly string at me, had champagne flutes, and began giving me hugs and handshakes congratulating me.

Was it my birthday?

No, my birthday wasn't for another 4 months. What the hell was going on?

Sarah then gave me a huge hug and filled me in,

"Sledge, Panoramic Records are fast tracking the record contract and tour! We showed them some recordings of your guys' rehearsal, they went ape shit, and want to sign you guys immediately!"

"We wanted to wait to tell you until everything was finalized and inked but the second you sign these documents; Virgin Sinner will officially be Panoramic Recording artists!"

Holy shit. I couldn't believe everything was happening so quickly! This was amazing! I excitedly asked,

"When do we begin recording the album and when does the tour start?"

Before giving me an answer, Sarah sat me down and had me quickly sign through our recording contract. It was a huge contract, but I was too excited to even care. She told me that most of it was just legal mumbo jumbo so I just had her show me where to sign and I signed it.

Hell yeah!

This was going to be awesome!

After I initialed the final page, she finally filled me in,

"Okay, well ever since we got the word from the grapevine that Panoramic were more than likely going to sign you guys, the band began recording their parts for the record. Literally everything is finished and all you need to do is perform your guitar parts and lead vocals, which will only take a few days. As for the tour, you guys are set to kick off in Kansas City in two weeks."

I asked,

"Is it normal for stuff like this to happen this quick out here?"

She replied,

"Oh, honey, this is Hollywood. 'Normal' isn't in our vocabulary!"

I chuckled,

"I see that! Okay. Wow. So, when do I start recording?"

She said,

"Everything is set up and ready to go right now if you want to get cracking on it!"

Her excitement was charming and only added to my then current state of cloud 9 I was floating on.

I gave Sarah a huge hug and thanked her from the bottom of my heart for helping make all my dreams come true. She gave me a kiss on the cheek and left. I genuinely liked Sarah. She was incredible at her job and great at keeping us all excited about what was to come.

At that point, it was time to knock out the debut Virgin Sinner record and rehearse our asses off for the big tour.

I ended up recording all my parts for the Virgin Sinner record in under three days. I was so well-oiled from all of our hardcore rehearsals that I almost nailed the whole damn thing in one take. It felt amazing.

We then began rehearsals for the tour, which included a kick ass stage set up as well as some special imported pyro that would make Kiss jealous. It was probably the busiest few weeks of my life and I didn't even have an opportunity to just take a step back and think about how wonderful everything was going.

After our second to last rehearsal before the tour, the car dropped me off at home and I was finally able to take a special moment to appreciate everything that was going on. I plopped down onto my bed and lay there with stars in my eyes just thinking about how I couldn't believe I was actually doing it.

As my brain began drifting off to sleep with the comfort of knowing that true success was just around the corner, my mind began shifting into empathy mode in regards to Robin. It filled my brain like a toxic virus as it usually did every night.

Was he okay?

Is he pissed at me?

Will he even let me help him?

I still wasn't able to find him even though I would take time after rehearsals to search for him. Nobody knew where he was. Mercedes hadn't seen him; nobody had. It was driving me crazy and I couldn't help but toss and turn.

As per usual, I eventually lied to myself to be able to drift off to sleep. I would convince myself that Robin was a big boy and was able to handle his situation on his own. I mean, I was in the big city and I had to start thinking like the big city folks instead of worrying so much about others. With this mindset, I was then able to fall asleep, finally.

I was laying in my bed in the pitch black darkness that was my room and from out of nowhere, I heard what sounded like heavy breathing. My eyes shot open but couldn't see anything. My black-out curtains were doing their job and I could tell no difference from when my eyes were open or closed.

I was conscious in a void it seemed. I was a little freaked out to say the least. My mind began racing and wasn't sure if I was either being burgled, or being tormented by the ghost of someone who used to live there.

I was frozen in fear.

The heavy breathing continued and morphed into a wheezing sound; it was almost inhuman. I then kept telling myself that I was only dreaming and that I would probably be waking up at any moment in a cold sweat attributed to my stress induced night terror.

The wheezing mutated into a high-pitched screech.

I pinched myself as hard as I could to wake up. I pinched so hard that my fingernails broke skin and could feel blood between my fingertips.

Oh fuck, I wasn't dreaming.

Still frozen in fright and hoping, praying, that whatever was in my room would go away, the high-pitched howl turned into a maniacal slow laughter. I was in a fever pitch of fear. I couldn't even scream if I wanted to.

Then the constant static of sinister laughter ceased. It was dead silent.

Did whatever it was go away?

My mind couldn't stop racing.

What do I do?

Eeriness overcame me as I still sensed a presence in my dead silent room. It felt like I had a pair of eyes on me with intent. It was a feeling I would never forget.

The silence broke with a feeble voice that vaguely sounded familiar,

"Was it all worth it?"

Silence then swallowed the moment following this cryptic statement from my unseen intruder,

"Was... it... all... WORTH IT?"

The voice repeated itself,

"Was it all worth it, Toby?"

"Was it ALL worth it?"

He knew my name. Then it clicked.

It was Robin.

"Robin?"

I gently said, breaking his vamp which continued even louder,

"WAS IT ALL WORTH IT?!"

I rolled off my bed and frantically felt around for the lamp in my room, knocking over everything in my way. After a few moments, I finally I found it and turned it on.

I immediately backed away, knocking over the lamp, after I had seen what became of Robin. The fallen lamp created an eerie luminescence to him and all I could do was stare in silence at what used to be my friend. If it weren't for his signature denim jacket, I would have never been able to recognize him.

His face was covered in sores, which were dripping with blood. His eyes and cheek bones were sunken in to the point his once good-looking face had caved in upon itself. His lips were almost non-existent as they looked like he had begun chewing them off.

He was hunched over and leaning against my dresser breathing heavily with bloody viscous drool falling out of his helpless mouth. He looked like Jeff Goldblum from The Fly. I frantically said,

"Robin, we need to get you to the hospital, man! Holy fuck! Come on dude, I'm taking you right now!"

I began to get dressed but Robin lurched toward me.

"Was it all worth it?!" he spit out of his now crooked mouth.

"I don't know what you're talking about man, but we need to leave, now!"

I frantically looked for my keys but my mini-mission was halted the second I heard a gun being cocked. I looked over at Robin and he had a pistol pointed directly at me with intent. His now jack-o-lantern of a face formed an evil grin,

"Was it all worth it?"

His demonic demeanor then vanished as he ceased pointing his pistol at me. He let out a whimper. It was as if he realized what he was doing and whatever was possessing him had let him go for a moment to tease himself with regaining his soul.

If his eyes could talk, they would be asking for help. It flashed me back to Grace, the first cow I killed at the slaughterhouse. It was almost the same look as if they knew they were too far-gone to do anything about their situation. My heart sank for Robin.

As I approached him to intervene, his inner demons put up their defense once again. His evil grin returned and I paused where I was standing; a good 4 feet away from him. He locked eyes with me and as a single tear fell from his broken face, Robin's real voice shone through with a single statement,

"You were never there to hold my hair."

Then in the blink of an eye, he pointed his gun to his own head and pulled the trigger.

At that exact moment, I knew that life itself would never be the same again.

9

THAT'S OUR BOY

AFTER AN EVENING OF being questioned by the police and turning down grief counseling, I was in an absolute haze. I couldn't shake the dark and twisted responsibility I felt for Robin's death. Not only was I chosen to take his hopes and dreams away but I played a part in his decision to take his own life away from himself as well.

Where do I go from here?

How do I bounce back from this?

I went to the convenience store to see Phil to break the news. He was the only real friend I had out here and the only one I could turn to.

As I walked into the store, Phil noticed right away that something was terribly wrong. He rushed over to me from behind the counter and said,

"Oh, what the hell happened, Toby? Are you okay?"

Due to the complex severity of the situation the only words I could muster up to blurt out was the cold hard bottom line,

"Robin's dead"

Phil stood there in shock for a moment.

"Oh god, what the hell happened? Was it the drugs? Wait, you knew Robin?"

I took a deep breath and filled him in on the dark and twisted situation. He was as. emotionally as shaken up as I was.

After a few moments of grieving, I inquired as to what I should do from that point forward. Should I go back home to Delane? Do I take a few weeks off from everything? I was lost in so many different ways.

Phil then hit me with some wonderful words as he usually did,

"All you can do is keep working, Toby. Work is good for the mind and soul and you need to keep doing what you're doing otherwise you're going to drive yourself crazy with guilt."

"You need to approach this band situation as more so a tribute to Robin now. You have to understand that this was not your fault in the slightest. That boy was on some serious shit as far as drugs are concerned and with the right concoction of chemicals and downer thoughts, it only becomes amplified and unfortunately in Robin's case it ended in suicide."

"You need to take this as a lesson, Toby; that it's okay to stick your hand in the fire to make sure it still burns every once in a while but don't crawl into hell and claim it as your new home, otherwise you'll end up just like Robin."

Phil's words resonated with me and actually made sense. There was no helping Robin and he had chosen his path.

I needed to stay focused.

I went home to go pass out from what felt like emotional and physical exhaustion. Fortunately, the police and forensics team were finished with their job and everything seemed back in order.

I couldn't fathom walking back into my apartment, the scene of the crime, but after multiple inquiries to move to a different room being declined due to no vacancy, I didn't have a choice and needed to face the situation head on.

No more than five minutes after I lay my head down, the phone rang,

"Hello?"

"Yes, Sledge, the car is out front to pick you up for rehearsal."

I was confused to say the least. I asked them if they were privy to the news of what happened to Robin. The monotone voice replied with,

"Yes. We know. The car is out front, we're on a tight schedule."

Click.

Was this just the way people in Hollywood dealt with suicide let alone death? Do the wheels in the sky really just keep turning like nothing happened?

I was so conflicted internally. Maybe this happened more often than people imagine it would out here. Maybe I was just thinking too much?

I put my thoughts aside, affirmed by the fact that I needed to keep working like Phil mentioned. I quickly got ready and ran down to the car.

I arrived at rehearsal and everyone seemed strangely calm as usual. I assumed the news had reached everybody already but I still felt the obligation to fill everyone in just in case,

"Did you guys hear about Robin?

Everyone just stared at me like I had nine heads. Our drummer Steven said,

"Yeah we know," then diverted with,

"Sledge, are you tuned up and ready to go?"

I took a deep breath,

"Yeah, I'm ready, but aren't you guys surprised or sad? I mean Robin came up with you guys."

He stared at me sternly but calmly said,

"We're not surprised at all. It sucks that it ended up happening in your apartment, but that's life in Hollywood, man. When the chips fall, there's no point in looking down and staring at them. You gotta pick up whatever you can and keep moving. We have a lot of work to do, so let's get on it."

This statement confirmed my big city assumption. I guess perhaps this was just a part of life out here.

At the end of our final rehearsal before the tour, Sarah informed me that Mr. Sayer himself wanted to have a meeting the following morning to go over very important details about my contract with The Agency.

Maybe everyone was right; I had to pick up what I could and keep moving. I needed to treat this as a tribute to Robin and I needed to keep working.

The thought of finally being able to meet the head honcho of The Agency gave me something new to look forward to. My mind was back on track as much as it could be.

The car brought me home as it had many times before and I climbed into my bed. Suddenly it felt like everything was back to normal in a bittersweet sort of way. I had all of my dreams imminently coming true and the butterflies in my stomach had returned.

Let's do this.

The next morning, I woke up to my phone ringing for which I picked up and proclaimed,

"Yep, car is waiting out front, Got it."

After all, The Agency were the only ones to ever call and it was always about the same damn thing.

I was looking forward to my meeting and the idea of having all my future plans and successes laid out before me had me giddy. I got off knowing that my musical abilities were finally going to be shown off plus the fact that one of the biggest agencies in the world believed in me; it felt like my whole existence was affirmed.

We arrived at The Agency Headquarters. I wasn't used to seeing architecture like that let alone be invited inside such a skyscraper of a building.

After walking through the lavish lobby, we entered the elevator. The driver took out a special key card, which took us to the top floor of the building. The door opened to not a waiting room, which I expected, but the office itself. It was a gargantuan conference room decorated with gold and platinum records and lined with shots of former and current rock stars, political figures, and other celebrities.

I was amazed and asked the driver,

"So, the Agency has worked with all these people?"

He replied with,

"Every single person on that wall owes every bit of their success to The Agency."

The light was dim in the large room and as we walked in, we approached a table that seemed to be as long as a locomotive. It was insane.

The office overlooked the whole city. It was beautiful. At the far end of the table, I saw a dimly lit figure sitting down. It was too dark to tell but I knew it was a person due to the fact that a breath of cigarette smoke had exhaled from the unseen man's mouth.

We approached closer and I could finally see his face. A distinguished older gentleman, I'd say mid-sixties with what looked like a very expensive haircut and a Vincent Price pencil thin mustache.

The monotonous sound of our approaching footsteps was broken by the deep bellowing voice of Mr. Sayer, which sounded like it could cut through anything,

"Ah. There's our boy! Sledge! As I live and breathe!"

To call him debonair would be an understatement. The man was full of playful class that I couldn't help but admire and enjoy.

Mr. Sayer stood up and approached me with his right hand outreached. I sank my palm into his for our initial handshake and his gorilla grip was impressive for a man his age. I greeted him with,

"It's so nice to meet you sir, I can't express how thankful I am for everything you're- "

He cut me off mid-sentence,

"Oh, save your thank yous for later, young man. Trust me, you're doing more for me than I'm doing for you."

The rush of meeting the man behind the orange curtain derailed any thoughts of confusion toward his comment; so I just shut up.

"Please, Sledge, have a seat."

We both sat down and I looked around his office; it was so vast and open. I noticed a sofa about 20 feet from where I was with a man sitting down facing me reading a book; although he held his book in his hands, he was staring directly at me with some sort of odd intent. It made me uncomfortable but curious.

He was a lanky fellow in a suit with glasses and was definitely younger than Sayer. He had an intense stoic face that never seemed to break. He didn't blink once either. Mr. Sayer broke the silence,

"Ah, where are my manners- Sledge, please meet Mr. Woods; my personal assistant."

I waved but Mr. Woods just continued to stare. Mr. Sayer explained,

"He means well, trust me. He's one of those people who are almost too good at their job, if you know what I mean. Mr. Woods is by all means a consummate professional."

The whole scenario felt a bit odd but I nodded at Mr. Sayer who proceeded to stare at me for a good moment. I flashed backed to my job interview with Mr. Goodman at the slaughterhouse and I reinvigorated my headspace with the fact that there was no situation I couldn't get through.

I mentally cleansed my palette and began humming "In-A-Gadda-Da-Vida" out of nervousness as I've done countless times before.

"Iron Butterfly!"

Mr. Sayer exclaimed,

"We had every bit to do with that band's success. Those guys did some great work for us."

He then diverted the conversation,

"I assume you know who I am and why you are here?"

I gathered my words for my reply,

"Yes sir. I am excited and honored."
Mr. Sayer smiled,

"Good."

He then drew attention to the paperwork in front of him,

"Okay, Sledge, time to get down to business. What I have in front of me is your record and managerial contract that you inked with us. I take it you read through everything?"

I sat there thinking for a moment then said,

"The Panoramic Records contract?

He laughed,

"Son, we *own* Panoramic Records. That wasn't just your record contract; that was your arrangement with us as a whole. Did you read it or not?"

I nervously replied,

"Well I was a little too excited to read through everything but Sarah told me that a lot of it was boiler plate legal stuff, so I just signed it to get it over with."

Mr. Sayer smiled,

"I am moved by your naivety. Truly. But in order for you to get a full grasp on what we're going to have you doing for us, you should really take a moment to read over the contract."

I looked down at the contract and it looked a few pages shy of a fucking phone book. It was enormous. In an effort to not have to spend the following 6 hours reading the giant contract, I replied,

"I write, record, tour and you guys market me. That's the gist of it right?"

"Not quite."

"I'm confused."

Mr. Sayer's smile grew larger,

"Are you ready to jump out of the frying pan and into the fire, young man?"

I had no clue what he was talking about. I started getting a little uncomfortable,

"I'm not sure I'm following what your hinting at, Mr. Sayer?"

He then looked behind me near the entrance of his office and stared for a moment. My unease was building even more. He motioned to the driver, who proceeded to roll something over covered in a black sheet and parked it into the middle of the office. It looked like a wheelchair.

"Okay, Sledge. It's now time for your first assignment."

I was beyond confused,

"Assignment?"

Mr. Sayer walked over to the wheelchair and ripped off the sheet. I was in absolute shock when I saw what was underneath.

It was Phil.

Unconscious.

Tied to the wheel chair.

Covered in blood as if he had been roughed up quite a bit. I squealed,

"What the fuck?!"

I was frozen in fear. I then felt a pinprick in my neck with a warm sensation that followed.

Before I could mutter my next words, I turned to see the blank faced Mr. Woods next to me who had just finished injecting me with a syringe full of unknown contents.

"Welcome to Hollywood, Sledge," proclaimed Mr. Sayer with a devilish grin,

"Enjoy your go-go juice. You should be getting the warm and fuzzies any moment now."

Before I could blurt out a word, my whole body began to fall into a state of intense euphoria. It felt like I could take on a whole army by myself but at the same time it felt like if I lay down, I could sleep for a thousand years.

What did they inject me with?

Mr. Sayer walked over to me and slammed a gun down onto the table,

"It's time to earn your keep, young man. You should have read your contract."

I couldn't speak. Sayer then sternly threw words at me through his grin,

"It goes like this; we give you everything you ever wanted and you give us what we need as far as tying up loose ends for The Agency. No questions asked."

I could feel my heartbeat pounding through every inch of my body. I began to sweat profusely.

Mr. Sayer smiled,

"I'd say get it over with before he wakes up."

A million emotions flooded through my brain. I sheepishly asked,

"Why Phil? What did he ever do? He's my friend!"

Mr. Sayer took a moment and prepared his words carefully,

"This man fed drugs to my previous golden boy to the point of him killing himself; In your apartment too I believe, correct? This thing sitting before us is a drug peddler, sex trafficker, and all-around piece of shit. He would have gotten to you too if he had more time, trust me."

I couldn't believe these words. Phil seemed like a genuinely wholesome human being! I mean, even if he did do those things, I could never bring myself to kill a man over it!

Mr. Sayer interrupted my thoughts with,

"Let me put it to you simply, Sledge. Either you put a bullet in this man's brain, or we put a bullet in your brain. Then we take a trip to Delane and put a bullet in everyone you've ever loved's brain. A love letter from you on behalf of the agency."

He then motioned to Mr. Woods who slapped the gun into my hand and walked me over to Phil.

I stood there and stared into oblivion for what felt like eternity.

Mr. Sayer continued,

"Oh, by the way, do you feel that? That's what we in Hollywood call speedball but our version has a little extra chemical oomph to it. Definitely not street-grade. You will feel intense energy, focus, and comfort all at the same time. A few more doses of this and you won't have any problems finishing any job we put in front of you."

Phil then slowly began waking up. His eyes filled with sorrowful tears and confusion once they connected with mine. Was he guilty of those awful accusations? It just didn't make sense to me. But at the same time, absolutely nothing made sense to me in Hollywood.

The feeling from the speedball fully kicking in and rushing through my veins activated some kind of primordial switch in my brain. I had officially snapped. At that moment, all I was able to hear over and over in my mind was,

"Kill, or be killed."

Phil began whimpering for his life and pleading with me, his friend, to help him,

"Toby, please! Help me!"

The rush inside my veins grew stronger and more intense which fueled me with a euphoric fuzzy rage.

The last thing I remember hearing before blacking out was two gunshots and the sound of Mr. Sayer's voice,

"That's our boy."

10

GOTTA KEEP WALKING

I WOKE UP ON what appeared to be some sort of private jet. I scanned around and noticed my band mates were spaced out on the almost empty plane sleeping. I then convinced myself that I had just awoken from the most vivid nightmare of murder. It made me feel loony tunes that my subconscious could come up with such a scenario.

I stretched out in my incredibly leisure sofa-like first class chair and relaxed for a moment. I figured we must have been on our way to kick off the Virgin Sinner tour. This was it. The big time, baby.

In the chair next to me I noticed a large black suitcase with a black duffel bag beside it. Upon further inspection, I saw that the suitcase had my name etched onto it; so I grabbed it, sat it on my lap, and opened it up.

Inside was a letter envelope on top of three large manila envelopes and some kind of odd container.

I opened the letter envelope and began reading its contents, which would confirm this nightmare to be all too real,

Dearest Sledge,

You have proven yourself to be an absolute rock star in more ways than one. We are all thrilled to have you a part of our team and are looking forward to much success on and off the stage with you.

In the suitcase in front of you, you will find three folders worth of information. While on tour, you are expected to execute each job within the timeline provided with each assignment. There are also strict instructions on how to dress each scene once finished.

In the glass case you will find a generous supply of your go-go juice, which will aid you with your hefty tour schedule and extracurricular activities, if you will.

All assignments and due dates have been perfectly routed to coincide with your tour schedule. We know what you are capable of and have no doubt that you will figure out a way to pull this off brilliantly.

Finally, in the black duffel bag, you will find your tools of the trade, which you will be responsible for.

Needless to say, everything you are being exposed to here is of the utmost confidential. Keep in mind, we will have eyes on you at all times so if you ever decide to resign from your position, you and you loved ones will be found and executed with extreme prejudice.

Above all, Sledge, have some fun. You will find this whole situation isn't as bad as you think.

Sincerely,

Robert Sayer

The Agency.

After reading the letter, my mind began to go into anxiety overload.

Fuck.

It wasn't a nightmare.

What had I gotten myself into?

Then, as if it were some kind of ghost like muscle memory to ease my brain, my hands dove for the container of go-go juice, cracked it open and shot up.

As the warm fuzzies flowed through my veins, all morality began to slip away with the realization that maybe the situation really wasn't so bad after all. I was sure people had done far worse for less. Plus, at the end of the day, I was about to explode into fame.

I looked down at the manila envelope that contained my first assignment and removed its contents. On top appeared to be a few candid photographs of a thuggish looking man in his mid-thirties whose name was Terrence Malvio.

Aside from the photos, name, and associated gang, which were called The Red Spider, all that was included in the package were various last known addresses as well as acquaintance addresses.

The final page was in its own envelope with the words,

Open immediately following assignment's dispatch.

The specific dispatch date listed was later that day. I guess it was time to get to work.

Our jet landed in Kansas City and my band mates didn't say much to me, which actually was a good thing because, by that point, I wouldn't even know what to say to them. We were almost over-rehearsed so I had no worries about the tour, which began in two days. The only worry on my mind at that moment was to rent a car and track down my first assignment.

After securing a rental vehicle, local map, and another hit of go-go juice, I, along with my duffel bag, began traversing through my first assignment's stomping grounds, which was a few hours from where we landed. I felt like a private detective. I felt pretty cool to be honest with you.

After a few dead-end inquiries around town, I finally stumbled upon my first real lead at Mr. Malvio's ex-girlfriend's apartment. She informed me that after a fight they had about his lifestyle, he would relocate to a local motel to carry on with his devious business of running drugs and women for sex trafficking.

The ex-girlfriend pretty much painted a vivid picture of this awful human being, which actually made me feel better about what I had to do to him. On top of everything else, he was a drug addict, an abusive husband and abusive father. It also turned out he was a major player in The Red Spider, the gang he was affiliated with.

I could only imagine why The Agency wanted him gone but at the end of the day, no questions asked, right?

I graciously took the motel's address from the woman and she left me with a few words,

"Whatever that bastard has coming to him, it's still not what he truly deserves."

I strolled back to my car and took a deep breath,

"Let's do this."

I drove over to the motel and parked. It was a sleaze ball of a joint. It was a two-floor complex with all the rooms overlooking the parking lot which made it easy for me to observe. By that point it was nighttime already with my deadline looming.

I took some time to witness the foot traffic in and out of certain rooms. Men greeting their affairs for dirty infidelity activities were very commonplace at this particular establishment it seemed. Although, one particular room caught my attention; instead of women going into the room for their paid 25-minute increments, women were being escorted out.

That had to be my guy.

I kept in mind which room it was and drove around back behind the motel; first floor and 4 rooms to the right. I parked my car in the vacant lot behind and grabbed my duffel bag. I crept up to the window of the room, which peered into the bathroom and beyond that I was able to view the rest of the room.

The bathroom light was off but there was one lamp on in the main room. After a brief glimpse, all I could see was a man in shorts, shirtless, and in a Mexican wrestling mask about to get down and dirty with one of his ladies.

Kinky.

Once they were out of view and audibly getting it on, I slid the window up and crept into the bathroom. I dug my hand into my duffel bag and pulled out what could be considered a small machete of a knife with rigid teeth. It was the weapon I was to use for this assignment.

Just as I was about to make my presence known, the woman barged into the bathroom and flicked on the light.

We locked eyes.

I was exposed.

Fuck.

At first, she was startled but then became angry. She looked behind her and yelled to her temporary companion,

"Hey, you know I'm going to have to charge you more for the extra company, right?"

Then I heard the man's voice,

"What the fuck are you talking about, bitch?"

Without thinking, I used the butt of my knife to incapacitate her.

The man heard her body fall to the floor and charged the bathroom. I widened my stance as much as I could and the second I saw the mass of the man coming toward me, I went at him and ran my knife directly into his neck. Blood painted the bathroom walls red and the man fell onto his back clutching his neck and gurgled his last breath before becoming an inanimate object.

Murder wasn't as hard as I initially thought. As long as I pretended I was back at the slaughterhouse and replaced people with cows, I figured the whole thing could work out just fine.

Plus, the drugs helped.

I took a moment to give myself another shot of my medicine and then dug into my duffel bag for my instructions as to what to do next with the body.

I opened the envelope, which revealed a startling depiction. It was a hand drawn diagram of what appeared to be a headless human. Each arm and leg were severed at the elbow and knee and sewed onto the man's midsection to create a twisted looking man-spider. Each of the man's eyes were removed from his head and placed onto his chest. There was a note at the bottom of this diagram, which said,

Required arrangement for assignment depicted above.

Bring remaining item to this location on the specific date listed:

1324 S. Belmont Pl.

Kansas City, MO

I assumed that the remaining item would be the man's head.

Any instance of morality was waned with my new favorite drug kicking me into gear. At that moment in time, my only concern was,

Where the fuck am I going to find a sewing kit?

But that issue was put to rest once I fished around my duffel bag and found a mini sewing kit along with a plastic tarp which probably would have come in handy a few minutes prior.

I dragged the man completely into the bathroom and got him into the bathtub. I figured that would take care of whatever excess blood I'd have to deal with from that point forward. I thought to myself,

All right Sledge, just keep thinking about the slaughterhouse and those hunting trips you went on as a kid. Humans are pretty much animals so it's no big deal.

As I began sawing the man's head off, the corpse came back to life and began to kick and gurgle.

Fuck!

He wasn't all the way dead!

My instincts kicked in which caused me to slam the blade of the knife through the Luchadore mask into the man's right eyehole down to the hilt which caused the scene to go silent and still.

Shit.

I needed to use both eyeballs for the final arrangement. I'll have to wing it.

I continued to saw the man's head off and his blood flowed down the drain in a steady stream. It was eerily quiet at that point and all you could hear aside from a pin drop was my knife sawing into meat coated bone, and blood swimming down the drain as if someone had just taken a shower.

After his head was completely detached, I took a smoke break and took a peek inside the mini-fridge of his room and noticed 4 beers left from a 6-pack.

Bingo.

I sat on the toilet and stared at the lifeless corpse in the bathtub for a moment. I made a toast,

"Here's to you, you sick son of a bitch. No, not you, you're the sick *headless* son of a bitch. I'm the sick son of a bitch."

It made me chuckle.

I took another shot of my medicine and got back to work. Once I finally detached the man's arms from the elbow down and legs from the knee down, I began sewing but stopped almost immediately.

I was stricken with a major issue that hit me upside the head like an epiphany. I couldn't believe what I was doing. I felt like I had failed at life at that particular moment. I then thought out loud,

"Wouldn't it make more sense to get all the pieces on the bed first *then* sew him together? It would be so much less strain on my back; after all, I have to perform on stage in two days and the last thing I wanna to do is throw my fucking back out."

I laughed at the adorably macabre nature of the situation and carried on.

I laid the tarp out onto the bed along with the man in pieces and after a good hour and a half of sewing his arms and legs to his torso, had created the man-spider. Which made poetic sense since the man was a major player in The Red Spider gang.

I finished up by plucking out his left eyeball and what was left of his right eyeball. I sort of added leftover sinew to his right eyeball to give it more mass since I destroyed most of it with my final kill stab. I smeared his body in his own blood to cap off "The Red Spider" effect and voila. I took a photo and began to exit through the bathroom and the feeling of idiocy washed over me.

I forgot the head.

I walked back toward my twisted piece of art and picked up the man's head. I grabbed it Lu-chadore mask first causing the beheaded domicile to slip out and fall to the ground. It was at that moment the true terror finally sunk in.

I killed the wrong man.

Shit.

What do I do?!

I took a moment to regroup and figure out
how the hell I was going to dress the scene then it
hit me. The hooker was still knocked out in the
bathroom.

Perfect.

I then began redressing the room accordingly.
I injected the passed-out hooker full of my go-go
juice, seeing as she would seem more drug ad-
dled than she actually probably was as well as the
fact that she would be asleep long enough to be
found like this.

Not only would I put the blame on her for my
mistake but also, she would be able to take credit
for what I was about to do to my actual mark.

I grabbed a few strands of her hair to plant at
the next scene and headed out the bathroom window.

I then noticed something was off.

Very off.

I took a look around at the vacant lot and
made a stark realization.

The fucking car was gone.

Goddammit.

Just another day at the office, right?

I'll worry about that later, I guess.

I took a look at the motel and realized the
room was supposed to be on the first floor and 4
floors to the left. I was never a math genius in

high school. I was not even sure if that was a math related problem but either way.

I peeked through the correct window and it was the same set up as the other room. All of the lights were off so I could only assume that the man was sleeping, which was good for me. I already had good practice with my previous folly and was ready to do it for real.

I took a hit of my go-go juice and realized it was the last hit that I had.

Great.

Once again, I convinced myself that I would worry about it later. I was good for the time being.

I slipped into the window, which led to the dark bathroom, and all I could hear was something fast moving through the air and the last thing I remembered was the sound of something blunt hitting my skull.

I came to and I was tied to a chair in the middle of the motel room.

What the fuck?

I then heard a voice but no one was visible,

"So, they sent you, huh?"

I felt a set of hands brushing through my hair,

"You're a pretty boy, ain't ya?"

I cringed with all my might.

"You're about to find out what we do to pretty boys where I come from. Trust me, by the end of it, you're going to be in love."

I tried to speak but it was prevented by the fact that I had duct tape wrapped all around my head. The man continued,

"But first, we need to give your nerves a little test run to get them conditioned to the pleasures your about to experience."

I struggled as hard as I could but my assailant of a mark punched me in the back of my head. Then all I could smell was cloves.

"You ever see that movie Marathon Man?"

Oh god.

I knew where he was going with the situation. He had clove oil, which was a numbing agent; it meant that he was about to do something very painful to me.

"I'll take your silence as acknowledgement."

The man then removed the duct tape from my mouth and before I could say a word, he forced my mouth open with some kind of wedge. I started to scream, which ended abruptly as he began to strangle me until my wind pipe was an inch away from collapsing.

Lesson learned.

How the fuck am I supposed to get out of this?

My hands were tied behind the chair and had no give whatsoever; same with my feet.

The man then picked a tooth, a molar, and with a rusty pair of pliers, began to poke and prod at it, almost playfully. By that point, my body and mind were prepared for whatever painful event that was about to occur; so much so that I couldn't feel a damn thing emotionally or physically.

He latched onto the molar with his pliers and began to slowly twist; so slow it was maddening. At first there was slight pressure, then the tooth's nerve began to make itself known. A white-hot sensation washed over me and I could feel my heart pumping through my eyeballs. The man playfully began to chuckle.

I then, very slowly, felt my molar being ripped out of my head; the pain was unlike anything I had ever experienced.

"Don't worry, the clove oil is just a tease. We're having too much fun without it. I want you to feel every little sensation."

The only thing my mind would let me think about, apart from the white-hot pain, was the behemoth roar of the crowd that I hadn't even played in front of yet. I still had a lot of life left to live and hadn't even experienced what all that trouble was for yet. I couldn't let this guy take my dreams away from me.

Within my struggle, I realized the back of the chair was slightly loose. I knew if I could muster up enough strength, I'd be able to break free. Shit. I guess those action movies have a little bit of truth to them as far as when the bad guy catches the good guy and the good guy is able to escape from a seemingly impossible situation.

But was I really the good guy though?

Of course I was.

"They say your body can't feel pain in more than one spot on your body at the same time. We're about to prove that fact wrong."

I heard something being plugged in behind me. It turned out to be a hair dryer.

What the fuck is he going to do with a hair dryer?

He then positioned it in front of my left eyeball.

Oh shit.

He then slipped something onto my eye to keep it open. It looked medical. Where did this guy get this stuff? This was like something out of A Clockwork Orange.

"Let's see how long it takes to turn your eye completely white with this. I don't know about you but I'm having a blast. Let's start on 'low' and take it from there, shall we?"

The man then began to full on laugh,

"Is it safe?!"

This dude was twisted.

The heat on my eye was deafening. The pain was deafening. All I could hear was a slight ringing in my ear and the roar of the crowd in my mind began to get louder and cheer, "Sledge! Sledge! Sledge!"

This ain't over.

This motherfucker is dead.

Then with all the might inside of my body, I stood up with all my force and much like the incredible fucking hulk, broke out of the braces on my hands and feet, which turned out to be simple zip ties. Nonetheless, I felt like a bad ass.

At first the man was in shock at my strength, all credit due to the go-go juice building up as kinetic force within my body, no doubt. Not to mention my mental audience of Sledge followers.

In the swiftest of moves, I managed to take out my eye forceps without causing damage and quickly grabbed the hair dryer from the man and proceeded to, for a lack of a better term, beat the shit out of him with it to the point the hair dryer was completely obliterated.

I then began to strangle him with the cord of the hair dryer and something that chilled my soul was the fact that the guy was laughing the whole time I was killing him. Down to his last breath, he had a smile on his face as if he was in love with the pain and the shift of dominance in the situation.

After I knew he was dead, I took a well-deserved breather and had a smoke break to take a moment to reflect on what the hell had just happened.

I killed the wrong guy, my car got stolen, I just got tortured, and now I gotta turn someone into a man-spider. Again. It was all worth it though.

Right?

I replicated the man-spider directions in my case file. I then sprinkled the hooker's hair onto his body and did an idiot check of the room to make sure I left nothing behind. I had the man's head in my duffel bag as instructed; I was all clear.

Not to mention, I successfully framed the hooker ever so brilliantly. When these assholes are found, for one, they were gonna think that this chick had some kind of connection to organized crime, and for two, the authorities and gang are going to think they had an extra member that they didn't have. The confusion was going to be glorious. But the less questions I asked the better, right?

It was then time to figure out how to get to where I needed to get to. I walked outside and just began walking. I was sure a bus stop or gas station would pop up at some point.

I just gotta keep walking.

11

WE'RE THE GOOD GUYS

AFTER WHAT FELT LIKE 6 months straight of walking, I finally came to, aside from the cashier, a deserted run-down gas station; probably in the middle of nowhere. I walked in, awkwardly nodded at the slacker looking forty-year-old cashier, and then bee lined it straight to the bathroom to clean myself up as to not look suspicious being that I had just committed double homicide.

Man. I just killed two people and framed a hooker for it. What have I gotten myself into?

As I washed the stain and smell of blood and gore off my hands, face, and body, I heard a commotion coming from outside the bathroom door. It sounded like the cashier was having words with someone.

Great. Now what?

I pressed my ear up against the door. I couldn't make out any words in particular, just harsh tones and loud voices, which escalated into objects being thrown about in anger. Then everything went dead silent after what sounded like a shotgun blast.

An eerily long pause filled the air, which was cut off by a raspy, stern, and almost playful sounding voice,

"Sledge, you can come out now."

Was this a trap?

Was the Red Spider Gang following me after I took out one of their homies?

What's going on here?

Through the door I yelled back,

"No habla inglais!"

Seriously? Was that the best I could come up with?

"Quit fucking around, Sledge, we've got a lot of work to do."

Okay, so obviously whoever this is must be on team Agency.

Just to be sure I yelled,

"Friend or foe?"

A moment passed, some rustling around the gas station ensued and the man finally replied with,

"Trust me, you've got no choice but to be my friend. Now finish spanking your monkey or whatever the hell it is you're doing in there and let's get moving."

I slowly opened the door and saw what could be described as a tall, wide, bearded, and dread-locked man pacing around the store grabbing random items with one hand while he held a shotgun with the other. He was full of slovenly grace.

I looked behind the register and saw the cashier; now missing a part of his head. The blood from the shotgun blast was still dripping down the walls. I asked,

"Was that entirely necessary?"

"Fuck him. The guy is a pedophile. Well, was a pedophile. Trust me, The Agency has tabs on every asshole around the globe and it just so happened this was one of them. There's never a too awkward of time to get a little practice in, you know what I mean?"

I stood there for a moment,

"No, I don't know what you mean."

The man then began walking toward me, almost in an intimidating fashion. I took a step back and began to flinch and close my eyes as he raised his right hand. I slowly opened my eyes and all I could see a few inches from my face was a giant drink carrier.

"Half ice with diet anything."

I stood there confused for a moment,

"Wait, what?"

"Just fill it up, we're running late. I grabbed you a couple cartons of cigarettes and I have more of your go-go juice too so no worries on that."

I stared at him with a blank face for a second,

"I am so confused."

He began to chuckle.

"Oh, it'll all make sense. We're gonna have a blast."

I then adhered to his drink request and walked over to the self-serve soda machine. I had so many questions but from what I figured; we were going to be spending enough time together to have them all answered. I asked,

"What about the body?"

"Oh, fuck him. We're gonna leave him. Trust me, the local authorities and families will probably be happy this piece of shit is dead."

"Alrighty"

He threw me the keys to his car and said,

"You're driving. Oh, and throw that head in the trunk, it's already starting to stink. I'll get it catalogued and sent off to where it needs to go."

"Alrighty."

"And stop saying alrighty!"

"Okee Dokey"

He chuckled.

Even though I had no clue who this man was, apart from his affiliation with The Agency, I was able to tell right away that he and I had clicked. He then handed me a hit of go-go juice and I liked him even more in that moment.

We walked outside, I took a look at the vehicle and I was instantly pissed but relieved at the same time,

"So, you're the one that stole the car?"

He laughed,

"I had to see how well you would react under pressure. You didn't do too bad. Apart from the fact that you killed the wrong asshole."

I was shocked,

"You saw all that?!"

"Of course I did. I'm here to protect The Agency's new investment."

We got into the car and we set off to wherever we were late too. I wasn't entirely sure yet. The man then handed me a map with routes laid out and red dots. He pointed to one specific red dot in relation to where we were and said,

"This is our first stop, make it happen."

He then reclined his chair and instantly passed out. I couldn't even get a single question in before he fell asleep! The anticipation was killing me to find out more about him.

After a few hours of heading to the first red dot on the map, my nameless co-conspirator came to after his nap and said,

"Good, we're making good time. You know I'm not going to shoot you if you go five or ten over, right?"

I then began asking my inevitable and burning questions,

"So, who exactly are you?"

Almost offended, as if I didn't already know who he was,

"I'm Bob. I thought you would have figured that out by now?"

I had to think for a moment and he definitely did not sound familiar at all,

"No man, I had no idea."

"Well those fuckers at The Agency always seem to purposely leave out important information for dramatic effect anyway so I'm not surprised."

He then fell silent as if the conversation was over. I broke the silence,

"So, Bob, who exactly are you?"

He took a big swig from his half ice and half diet drink,

"Your babysitter."

I was actually pretty relieved at this revelation, to be honest. At least I had someone with me to let me know if I had the right victim or not,

"Well that doesn't suck."

He then began to eyeball my driving speed,

"Alright, pull over. You can tell a lot about someone by how they drive and from what I see, you like to play it a little too safe and not take as many chances as you should. So, with that said, I'm fucking driving now until you earn back the privilege, alrighty?"

I was taken aback by his forwardness. This must have been more of that west coast hospitality I was still getting used to,

"Okee dokey"

Bob chuckled.

We switched and he began driving,

"You know you fucked up back there big time, right?"

I didn't understand,

"What, with not going as fast as you wanted?"

"No, back at the motel."

I was perplexed.

He continued,

"I came close to having to intervene but wanted to see whether or not you had the balls to at least try and clean up your mess. Which you did."

I replied with,

"Well yeah, I mean I had a lot riding on this and I didn't want to be fucking up right out of the gate. It's bad enough I have to cope with the fact that I now have to kill for a living in order to fulfill my dreams and goals."

I was cut off abruptly by obscene laughter from Bob and said,

"What? What's so funny?"

He was still laughing but then formed words,

"You all start off the same. All of you."

"How so?"

"Well you pretty much sell your souls for fortune and fame and your heads are so far up your asses to realize the kind of shit your truly tied into. But that's okay. Ignorance is bliss."

I quickly shot another question at him,

"How do you tie into all this? How did you become involved?"

He sat silent for a moment but then finally replied,

"I don't think there's enough miles or time on the roads in all of the continental U.S. for me to dive into that one, buddy. Just know that I've been doing this a very long time and that you're lucky to have me with you and not one of the other scumbags Mr. Sayer usually assigns people. I actually have some personality if you haven't noticed."

He was definitely right about that one. The guy was nuts but in a fun way. I also noticed he had his left turn signal on for about 25 minutes.

I asked,

"What exactly does The Agency do?"

He prepared the right words in his head and replied with,

"We tie up loose ends for the betterment of our company and the world."

I still didn't understand and really wanted some answers. I also needed some more go-go juice.

"Bob, I obviously am in as far as I am right now and all I am asking is just for a little insight as to what exactly The Agency is all about. I mean, I haven't exactly had an opportunity to sit down and ask these questions seeing as I've been too busy being forced to kill people."

Bob thought for a moment then said,

"All you need to know is that we have been around for hundreds of years and we purely operate to rid the world of the scum of the earth and to even give back a little as well. Like you, you're being exploited for your talents but at a price, know what I mean? You're getting what you want and we're getting what we want. You were handpicked."

I sat there for a moment then replied,

"Okay. But handpicked? I don't get it?"

"Okay so we have sleeper agents literally all over the world and we operate on tips we get in from them as far as future employees or clients.

Remember all those pictures of celebrities and important figures at Mr. Sayer's office?"

"Yeah."

Bob continued,

"Okay, so every one of them has ties to us. They have worked for us in exchange for what they have. So now you see what you're being groomed for? Nobody makes it without going through us. Pop culture is our market and pop culture icons are the ones least bit to be expected to be murderers, but that's how they got there."

"So, I'm in this for life? And if I don't obey, The Agency kills my family?"

Bob laughed,

"Did you not read your fucking contract?"

I just stared at him for a moment.

"Ugh. Didn't think so. Okay, stated in your contract is an exclusivity clause to us for five years. Then you are up for renewal. We own you for that amount of time. As long as you keep doing what you're doing for us, then everything is fine; sure, your family is leverage against you but once you get into the spotlight on this tour, then trust me, it's all going to be worth it and will make sense."

"We wouldn't have chosen you if we didn't think you could handle it. Your background at the slaughterhouse, your talent, etc. you know how to kill and you know how to rock. One hand washes the other, know what I mean?"

I asked,

"Okay, so obviously you guys found me through that festival I played but how did you know about the slaughterhouse?"

Bob laughed,

"Okay, so full transparency on the table, you had a sponsor before you were chosen. Like I said, we have sleepers all over the world always on the lookout for our next employee."

"Who was my sponsor?"

Bob looked at me for a moment then said,

"Hans."

I was blown away,

"Hans, the old guy that ran the music store in Delane?!"

"Yep! You'd be impressed with how much work Hans had done for us while he was an active employee. He was a bad motherfucker. Oh! On top of that, that festival you played? We literally put that whole event together just to get you excited and to whisk you away to us."

"We love employing touring musicians because we can literally route a tour to where we need things taken care of. One big murder tour."

I sat there in shock for a moment then asked,

"I still am having trouble wrapping my head around this whole thing. So, you guys fabricate everything? Even huge events like that festival? What else have you guys done that I would know of?"

Bob replied,

"Okay, let me tell you a little story. You remember hearing about that Jacobstown Massacre some years back?"

"Of course, that was absolutely insane! The Agency had something to do with that?"

"That was considered one of The Agency's finest moments, man."

Confused, I asked,

"How so?"

He then filled me in,

"Okay, so that Jeff Jacobs cult leader asshole? He was actually working for us but he thought we working with him to feed into his fucked up religious cult. But in actuality, we were actually using him to convert people that we needed off the grid, if you know what I mean."

"It took many years to pull the trigger on that one. We gave him the resources he needed to pull in and convert a few thousand people on our shit list into his South American religious camp; drug lords, pedophiles, rapists, etc."

"By us feeding into his religion and his penchant for a mass suicide event, he managed to not only kill about a thousand people that we needed dead but he ended up offing himself as well which saved us the extra hassle."

"I remember being one of the first people down there to have to identify every one of those people to report back confirmation of their deaths to The Agency. It was a fucking nightmare."

"The one thing I remember the most was the smell in the air. You see, we weren't able to get down there until about two days after the job was done so the bodies were decomposing in the overwhelming South American heat and were filling up with maggots. The second I stepped out of the helicopter; I was instantly sick after I was hit with that first gust of maggot wind."

"Man, it was a tough job but we got it done. Everybody involved in that operation got promoted to the moon. So as bad as we may seem, we are ridding the world of douche bags to not only our benefit, but the world's benefit as well."

"We feed into what we need to as long as it makes sure the job gets done and you, sir, have all the drive in the world to be a famous musician that, to be perfectly blunt, we are using against you to do our work. How's that for transparency?"

I sat there for a moment to compute the story and situation. As with a trend in my life leading up to that moment, maybe ignorance really was bliss? Maybe the less I knew the better off I really was?

After all, there was an underlying 'doing the right thing' vibe with the whole thing even if it involved murder. But at the end of the day, The Agency was getting what they wanted and I was getting what I wanted.

After a moment of silence and in need of reassurance, I asked,

"So, we're the good guys?"

Bob took his eyes off the road to look me dead in the face and say,

"You're damn right we're the good guys."

12

ONE BIG MURDER TOUR

AFTER A NAP WHILE Bob was driving, I woke up in time to watch the sunrise. That particular sunrise felt a bit different than the ones I was used to in Delane. I couldn't tell if I liked them more or less with what they represented. For that moment, they represented another day of murder but I was hopeful that after that particular day, the sunrise would remind me of another sold out show. Which was where I couldn't wait to be.

That night was the kick off to our tour. I was having trouble wrapping my head around the whole thing still but I kept my inquisitive nature to myself at least for the time being. I had to keep reminding myself that we were the good guys.

I looked over at Bob and asked,

"How are we looking?"

"About 30 miles out. You know what you have to do right?"

After looking through my portfolio for a moment, I glanced over at Bob and said,

"Yep, as ready as I'm gonna to be."

The rest of the car ride to my next assignment was a comfortable silence. No radio, nothing. Just the sound of the tires rolling against the road to get to my next destination.

We began to roll into a heavily populated metropolitan area with many tall buildings. It was then I realized I once again had my work cut out for me seeing as my next mark was a sleazy lawyer named Ronald Kovis who worked in a very fancy law firm.

According to the portfolio, the guy was your typical loser with gambling debts up to high heaven on top of having children he didn't pay child support for and an ex-wife who would sleep more comfortably at night knowing that this vile human was eradicated.

Aside from owing money to everybody and taking bribes to throw court cases, he also ran a snuff film ring where he would desperately try to earn extra money to pay off his debts.

But as with any addiction, the second he would be positive in his checking account, the money would already be spent by placing bets all around town to whomever would take them.

Apparently, his ex-wife had ties to The Agency and Mr. Sayer had bought his debt with a deal in place where we would take care of Kovis and his substantial life insurance policy his ex-wife took out would not only clear his debts but allow his ex-wife and kids to live a comfortable life that they very much deserved.

With that knowledge, I felt like a superhero and could not wait to get to work knowing that even though it was murder, nobody was going to miss Ronald Kovis and it would be benefiting a good family in the end.

We pulled up to the entrance of the building where his law film resided and before Bob dropped me off in front he said,

"Alright, Sledge. Try not to fuck this one up as much as you fucked up the last one. I will be back here in thirty minutes to pick you up and if you're not here at that time, then have fun getting to the gig on your own."

I nervously chuckled but wasn't entirely sure if he was serious or not. Before I could even ask, he grabbed my arm, shot me full of my medicine and urgently barked,

"Get going! Hurry the fuck up!"

I then jumped out of the vehicle and looked up at the giant business building that stood before me. Was it bad that I wasn't entirely certain what city I was even in at that point?

I entered the building and bee-lined it to the information desk and told the clerk,

"Hello, yes, I have an appointment with Mr. Kovis today."

The old lady clerk then looked down at the meeting schedule and without looking back up at me said,

"Name please?"

Shit. I forgot the name that the appointment was under.

It was David something.

David White?

David Brown?

David something.

What the hell was it?

Without thinking I blurted out,

"It should be under David."

The lady continued to look down for a moment to scan through the appointment list.

"Benjamin David for Ronald Kovis? Right on time."

Damn that was smooth. She gave me his floor and office number. He was on the 46th floor. It was going to take me at least 5 minutes alone to make it up there and thinking about what Bob had said about not being back at the front of the building in thirty minutes had me anxious.

I hopped in the elevator, which felt like it was slower than molasses. With everyone getting on and off it took an extra 10 minutes to get to the 46th floor. There was no way I was going to have enough time to take care of Kovis and make it back down in front in fifteen minutes.

After traversing the 46th floor for a few moments, I found Kovis' office. I rang the buzzer and was buzzed in. The receptionist answered,

"He's expecting you, go right in Mr. David."

She pointed toward the door to his office.

I walked in and there he was, just like in his portfolio. Late forties, dressed nice but with an emptiness in his eyes. As the door shut, I walked toward him for a handshake and he said,

"Mr. David! Thank you so much for considering my legal expertise, we are all very-"

His sentence was then interrupted by the bullet from my silencer ripping through his face.

As his body hit the ground, still twitching, I shot off one more round into his forehead. Yep. He was dead. I looked at my watch and realized I had five minutes to get back down to the front of the building and knew there was no way I would make it.

Was Bob even serious about that? I had some quick thinking to do but came up with something so crazy that it might just work.

I exited Kovis' office with Kovis. I had his leg tied to my leg to make it seem like he was walking with me and had my arm around him to keep him propped up. We looked as if we were old buddies.

I had his hat on his head, which covered up his gunshot wounds. It was like something out of Weekend at Bernies. The receptionist looked at us oddly and I stated,

"We're going to go grab lunch and will be back in forty!"

I then did my best to awkwardly walk us both out of the receptionist area together. The second we made it out and the door shut, I looked both ways and saw nobody coming. I grabbed him by his belt, tossed him over my shoulder, and quickly headed past all of the other offices to the stairwell.

Just before I had my hand on the door to the stairwell, the closest office door opened and out walked what looked like a small group of lawyers. Kovis was slumped over my shoulder and I locked eyes with the small group of men for a good few moments. I quickly answered the question they didn't have to ask,

"Food poisoning and motion sickness, going to have to take him down the stairs."

I nervously chuckled at my statement. The men stared at me oddly then began to scream and scramble. As it turned out, at that precise moment, Kovis' hat decided to fall off revealing half of his head missing.

Fuck.

I ran into the stairwell and prayed that my plan would work. I had three minutes to make it down to the front of the building.

I propped Kovis on top of the railing and peered down into what looked like a bottomless pit to the ground floor. I then jumped onto Kovis' back and down we went. If my plan worked then Kovis' body would break my fall once we hit the bottom.

Although it would only take a few seconds to reach the bottom, everything felt like it was in slow motion. I looked around me and watched each landing pass floor by floor. I even made eye contact with a group of people smoking outside of one door. I looked down and finally was able to see the ground approaching quicker and quicker. Then it hit me,

Was this even going to work?!

Oh shit!

Then in a flash, Kovis' body exploded the second we hit the ground. I had no injuries what so ever. Apart from being covered in blood and gore, all I could think to myself was,

I can't believe it worked!

Good to know!

I tried to clean myself off as good as possible but as I looked up from the bloody pulpy mess, I realized that I was surrounded by about twenty office workers on their smoke breaks. They were also covered in Kovis' blood from the fall. We all stared at each other for a good moment and all I could blurt out was,

"Uh. Food Poisoning?"

A woman began to scream so I got the fuck out of there and ran outside to the front of the building as fast as I could. I looked down at my watch and still had one minute to spare.

Where the fuck was Bob?!

Aside from being in a busy public place in broad daylight covered in blood with my wheel man nowhere in sight, things got even more complicated once I began hearing police sirens. Cars began to screech to a halt all around me so I did the most logical thing in that moment. I ran up to a random car, a station wagon, pointed my silencer at the driver and said,

"Trust me, I need this car more than you do right now."

I never saw a man move so fast. I hopped in and floored it. Blinking lights far behind me then caught my attention. Great. The cops were on my tail.

At that point I was happy for all those times I snuck out and wreaked havoc with my father's truck in our neighbor's cornfields because as of that moment, I needed every bit of driving skill I could muster up.

I began running red lights and was praying that I wouldn't get sideswiped. Cars were screeching all around me and crashing into each other. It was like a Charles Bronson movie.

As the police made their pursuit, there must have been four squad cars. I quickly drove into an alleyway; I was scraping and bouncing off of everything on either side of me.

I popped back out onto the other side of the alley into another busy street and the cops were still on me. I couldn't shake them; I should have stolen a faster car.

I had one idea and it had to work otherwise I wasn't getting out of there. I sped up as hard as I could and the cop cars mirrored my acceleration. I was going so fast that the car felt like it was about to explode.

I waited for the right moment and distance between myself and the nearest police car behind me. I slammed on the brakes as hard as I could which caused the cop car behind me to rear end me and giving me a little accelerated boost once I floored it again.

I peered behind me and saw every cop car, every car really, piling up onto each other creating a sort of blockade of disaster. I saw this as my opportunity to escape and got the hell out of there.

I got as far away from that scene as quick as I could. The second I hit cornfields, I drove into the fields until I knew the car wouldn't be visible as a way for me to buy some time to commandeer another vehicle; hopefully one that wasn't a station wagon.

Being able to gather my thoughts, all I could think about was how pissed at Bob I was for not being there. I had one minute to spare! Was it a set up? What the hell was going on?

After about an hour on that empty road and with no cars coming from either direction, I at least felt at ease knowing that if the authorities hadn't caught up to me by that point, that I was going to be in the clear.

After walking for a while, I came across a small pond where I was able to wash off the rest of Kovis' blood. If I wasn't such a frantic mess at that point, I probably would have got some fishin' in.

It was hot enough outside to where my clothes dried pretty quickly so after few minutes I was almost back to looking as normal as humanly possible. I sat on the side of the road just waiting for someone, anyone, to come through so I could, naturally, frighten them with my gun and steal their car.

My drugs were wearing off and Bob had my refills so I wasn't feeling too good at all, which made me even more pissed at Bob.

I began to shiver from the withdrawals and my mental state was hardly cheerful or competent at that point. Not to mention, the kick off show for the tour was later that night. But finally, after what felt like hours, I could see a car up in the distance making its way down the old road.

As the vehicle, a Ford Escort, got closer, it began to slow down and eventually come to a stop a few feet in front of me. Its driver was a man who looked to be in his mid-thirties who was well dressed and well composed. He got out of the car and asked, with concern in his voice,

"You alright buddy? You need a lift?"

I thought for a second,

If this guy was into giving me a ride vs. me waving around my gun to steal his car, I should probably take the path of least resistance here.

I told him that my car was broken down further up the road and that I in fact needed a lift to Kansas City. He motioned for me to get in and off we went.

The man then began small talk,

"You know, you're lucky I came along this way, people hardly ever do; and with how hot it is outside, who knows how much longer you would have lasted out here."

I replied with,

"I really appreciate you picking me up, man. Who knows how long I would have been out here. What's your name?"

He looked to me and said,

"Bruce, and yours?"

"I'm Toby."

Bruce smiled and said,

"Well it's very nice to meet you Toby."

He then locked all the doors and flashed his badge,

"Oh, by the way, you are under arrest, Toby."

13

POLICE ESCORT

AS I SAT IN THE holding cell by my lonesome, I reflected on what had just happened. It turned out, Bruce was an undercover cop in some Podunk district of some corn field town that happened to have gotten the call that a man with my description was wanted for murder and major property damage.

Well played, Bruce. As if my withdrawal symptoms weren't bad enough, I was going to probably be spending the rest of my life in prison.

Would The Agency get me out of prison? I didn't even care anymore. I took the chance and went out to Hollywood with glitter in my eyes and signed a contract I should have read. I guess the only thing left to do was be accountable.

It was a tiny police station. There were maybe about 20 or 30 people working there; if that. I didn't even know where the hell I was in the country but it was definitely a small town, I knew that much.

I was interrogated for what felt like days. I kept my mouth shut about The Agency and I pretty much played the whole 'wrong place wrong time' card. They weren't buying it.

At the end of it, they pretty much told me that I was being convicted of Kovis' murder and that in a few hours I would be transported to Kansas City for my sentencing.

Kansas City. That's where my first show was supposed to be; later on that day actually. The thought crossed my mind to figure out a way to escape out of there but I had nothing. I had no ideas. I had no mojo. I was done. Defeated.

I couldn't believe Bob fucked me over like that. I was probably already off The Agency's grid by that point; expendable and left to die.

I mean, was I not good enough? It was nice to know I would end up spending the rest of my life in prison with all those awful questions festering in my brain. The rest of my life would be me obsessing about what could have been. My destiny had been demolished.

The police station was so small that I was the only prisoner. The place was like something out of Andy Griffith. My cell was removed from the main area, as they usually were, and it was dead silent. So silent it was deafening. All I had in my six by eight coffin was a broken toilet and a cot that felt like it was made out of concrete.

Was suicide an option? Probably not. As hopeless as I was, I still enjoyed existing, I guess. I decided to hop into my concrete bed and try and sleep to get away from being trapped inside my head.

My few minutes of somewhat peaceful slumber was obliterated by the sound of a thunderous gunshot.

Then another.

And another.

I woke up and the power had been cut off. It was pitch black. The voices of people yelling, screaming, and pleading were the only things I could make out between the shots.

What the hell was going on?

I peered through my cell into pitch black nothingness that was lit up every few seconds by shots fired. Eventually, the screaming became less and less seeing as their voices and lives were no doubt ended by some unknown assailant with what sounded like a big ass gun.

Silence then returned to the police station which lined up well with the pitch black to create a void of confusion. Suddenly, the power came back on. Was I dreaming? Was it apart of my withdrawal systems? I'd be lying if I said I didn't have butterflies in my stomach at the thought of learning more about what exactly was going on. My morbid curiosity was at a fever pitch.

The lights returned and the door leading to the cell area crept open. All I could hear were very slow but evenly paced footsteps. Who was it? Was I next? Was it some crazy redneck with a vendetta against the local middle-of-nowhere police station?

The unknown assailant then slowly came into view and made eye contact with me. He looked absurdly familiar. I had seen him before. He was dressed nice, had glasses, and had an almost awkwardly cool demeanor about him. Then it clicked.

It was Mr. Woods. The guy who kept staring at me in Mr. Sayer's office. What the hell was he doing there?

"Mr. Woods, right?"

He remained silent and just stood before me with his shotgun in hand staring at me like he did in Mr. Sayer's office.

"Am I getting out of here? Or am I a loose end to tie up?"

He then stomped his foot which made me shut up immediately.

After a few more moments of him uncomfortably staring at me, his monotone face smiled. He reached into his suit jacket pocket and handed me a letter. It was from Mr. Sayer,

Dearest Sledge,

It has come to my attention that you were in need of a get out of jail free card. Don't get used to this kind of treatment because everybody gets 'one'.

From what I understand you have a show tonight. Mr. Woods will be kind enough to escort you to the gig and where you will also handle your third assignment.

We are not in the business of fucking up, Sledge. Don't forget about what happened to Robin.

With that said, have a great show!

P.S.

Just know we have eyes on your family as we speak.

Mr. Sayer.

After a long and uncomfortably silent car ride with Mr. Woods, we entered Kansas City; which oddly looked familiar. After heading into the metropolitan area, it then struck me with shock that it was where I had killed Kovis and had my police pursuit. I should have paid more attention in Geography class in High School.

Hey, I was pretty good at rocking out and murder but never claimed to be a genius of academia. Get off my back.

Caution tape, ambulances and fire trucks were still present from my earlier situation. I was in Kansas City that whole time. I still couldn't wrap my head around that notion and realized that I should probably take in my surroundings a little bit better during future endeavors. After all, Bob was driving and knew where to go and I didn't care enough to actually take a look at where we were going. I just saw red dots on a map.

Speaking of Bob, where the hell was that son of a bitch?

We arrived at the venue for the gig which was a very nice theater. The butterflies began fluttering in my stomach again. It was time to finally let loose and have some fun.

Let's do this.

We pulled behind the theater and Mr. Woods pointed at the door for me to enter. I got out of the car and the mysterious man proceeded to drive off into obscurity.

I must say though, the fact that Mr. Woods was able to take out a whole police station with a shotgun definitely made him a consummate professional. A straight up bad ass.

I walked in and the first person I saw backstage was Bob.

Time to get some answers from this asshole.

We locked eyes and as I began darting toward him, he began yelling,

"You fucking idiot! I had us a police escort for the show and you thank me by destroying half the city? What the fuck is wrong with you?!"

That turned the whole situation on its head a little bit. I replied,

"You never mentioned we would have a police escort! Another one of those important pieces of information that purposely gets left out for dramatic effect I'm assuming?!"

He shot back with,

"Well had you read the whole fucking portfolio you'd have known that we were only about ten minutes away from the gig and that we would have a police escort! This was supposed to be one of the easy assignments, you jagoff!"

"Instead you went rogue, wreaked havoc, got arrested and taken to one of the few isolated police stations that The Agency has no influence on. Which is one big migraine headache for all of us because Mr. Sayer had to send in Mr. Woods and nobody likes being around that creepy unpredictable fuck."

Well shit. I guess *I* was the asshole in that situation. Maybe ignorance wasn't bliss after all?

"Sledge, just go get ready for the show. You already missed fucking sound check like the newbie that you are. Oh, and please for the love of rock n' roll, please read the next portfolio, like right now. It's in your dressing room."

I nodded and then confidently began walking away in a certain direction and halted when realized I had an important question to ask Bob,

"Uh, Bob. Which way is my dressing room?"

He pointed into the opposite direction I was heading,

"That way. Dumbass. Hurry up!"

I shot back with,

"Okey Dokey."

Bob chuckled and grimaced at those words as he always did but it was turning into *our* 'thing'.

I entered my backstage dressing room and it was very luxurious. Fully stocked fridge full of booze, deli trays, stage clothes and a whole bag of my beloved go-go juice. I said to myself,

"Man, if I had my go-go juice in that police station, I probably wouldn't have needed Mr. Woods."

A voice then broke my train of thought,

"You do realize that your go-go juice is just a placebo, right?"

I turned around and Mr. Sayer was standing there. Between him being in my dressing room and the reality of what my go-go juice actually was, my brain completely broke. I didn't believe it. I asked,

"Wait, what? No way, it couldn't be. Also why are you all the way out here?"

Mr. Sayer laughed and said,

"Sledge, I never miss any of my clients first public appearances. It's a way of showing my appreciation. As for your go-go juice, yes, it was all in your head this whole time."

I was stunned,

"What do you mean it was all in my head?"

Mr Sayer then laid the knowledge down on me,

"You see Sledge, you had it all in you all along. The juice was just a mental crutch for you to trick yourself into using your primal instincts. Your wit and strength all belong to you, not the juice. The juice is just water. So, if you got anything out of it, it was hydration if anything."

"As for the withdrawals? You would be impressed with what your mind can trick your body into feeling. Now relax for a few and go over the next assignment, we have a lot riding on tonight."

Mr. Sayer then exited my dressing room and I was still in shock over the fact that the go-go juice was a sham but at the same time I was impressed with the fact that I was able to do all of these otherworldly things on my own. I was like a fucking superhero. My confidence level then shot up to one hundred percent and things were feeling pretty damned good.

I grabbed the manila envelope out of my duffel bag, which thankfully re-appeared in my dressing room; thanks to Bob probably seeing that I left everything in our vehicle. Maybe that Bob dude ain't so bad after all.

I plopped down on the nice leather couch and before I was able to start reading the assignment, I heard a knock at the door,

"Come in", I said.

In walks an older man who reeked of sleaze but what else was new. He said,

"Hey Sledge! I'm Kevin Reigns, promoter of this venue and event tonight, and I just wanted to extend a hello and thank you for performing here. Your debut single has been on fire and racing up the charts and we are expecting a sold out show tonight. Congratulations on your success."

I looked down for a moment to soak in that new piece of knowledge. I had a single racing the charts? Things were really starting to look up! Wow! Then as I focused in on the photo for the assignment, I muttered out loud,

"Ah shit!"

Kevin reacted,

"I'm sorry is something wrong?"

I looked back up and said,

"Oh no not at all! Thank you so much for your kind words and we can't wait to tear the roof off of this place!"

He smiled, nodded, and as he exited said that if I needed anything, just to come find him. I stared at the photo of my assignment again and couldn't believe it.

I had to kill Kevin Reigns the concert promoter who just gave me compliments. It said that he was responsible for the local heroin epidemic and like many others, had a hand in sex trafficking, amongst other things.

As for directions for dispatchment, the portfolio left it pretty vague. It just said that I needed to have him dead by 8pm. Our set started at 8pm. I looked at the clock and it was 7:45pm.

Fuck.

I had fifteen minutes to figure out how to kill Kevin.

14

OPENING NIGHT

I EXITED MY DRESSING room and heard the opening band performing. Their singer introduced their encore which meant it was their final song then it was time for the switchover for my band to begin our set. I began to sweat profusely.

My first instinct was to go to my go-go juice but apparently that did absolutely nothing other than keep me hydrated so I had to think and I had to think fast.

I peeked through the curtain and it was without a doubt a sold-out show. At least four thousand people. Our single really must have been blowing up but I couldn't even enjoy that moment because I was too busy frantically trying to figure out how to stealthily murder someone.

Looking around the crowd, I noticed something that made my heart sink into my bowels.

In the front row I saw Mr. Sayer standing next to my mother, sister, and father with Mr. Woods standing on the opposite end of them. Oh god. Was it some kind of insurance policy to make sure I got the job done? Or was it just a kind gesture of surprise for the kick off of my tour and success so I could experience it with my family?

I didn't have time to ponder or think about that. I couldn't take any chances. I had to find Kevin and dispatch him immediately.

As I was peeking through the curtain and trying to avoid the fact that my family was there, I looked around the stage and created a lay of the land. Taking everything into consideration how I could off Kevin by the time our set began, which was about 10 minutes from then, I had a plan. I was just hoping that it fucking worked.

I was then whisked away by stage handlers and crew to get me ready for our first show together as a band. My band mates walked past me as I was heading into my dressing room to quickly change into my stage clothes and our drummer, Steven, snarled at me and said,

"Thanks for being there for us for sound check, Axl! We appreciate it!"

Normally a comment like that would bother me and make me feel bad but I had other fish to fry at that moment. As long as I stuck to my plan, everything should work out fine.

I got changed in my dressing room, and looked in the mirror to psyche myself up. I had everything on the line at that particular moment and failure was not an option.

Bob came in to give me a quick pep talk which consisted of,

"Alright Sledge. I'm going to tell you three very special words that when joined together creates an incredibly powerful and important statement that will echo throughout the rest of your life;"

"Don't. Fuck. Up."

I nodded then casually asked why my family was there for which he replied,

"Oh great, you ruined the surprise. You better work your magic and work your magic fast because I still see that Kevin guy walking around and with Mr. Sayer and Mr. Woods tending to your family, well, let those three words I just said sink in and sink in good;"

"Don't. Fuck. Up."

"Got it?"

I nodded assuredly as he exited.

Alright, Sledge.

Let's do this.

We had about five minutes until show time and I hunted down Kevin to ask him to make sure he watched our show from stage left because of concerns with our pyro and other potentially dangerous parts of our stage show. He enthusiastically agreed and mentioned how excited he was for our set.

We were going on in a few moments and if all went well, then everything should fall into place perfectly.

My heart was racing. It was pounding so hard you could sample it and turn it into a Nine Inch Nails song. I had my guitar strapped on and ready to go. I peeked through the curtain one more time; the house lights were on and there was a buzz in the air for us. I spotted my family in the front row again and that time, Mr. Sayer and Mr. Woods made eye contact with me.

As they stood on either side of my family, Mr. Sayer smiled and proceeded to look over to Mr. Woods who casually opened up his suit jacket to reveal his shiny silencer pistol. The stakes were incredibly high and I had no choice but to prevail.

The house lights dimmed and our intro music began. Stage crew with flash lights guided me over to my area of the stage which was dead center. The house lights blinked on and off with certain parts of our intro music and during one of the lit moments I noticed Kevin, stage left, exactly where I needed him.

I looked to the front row during another one of the lit moments and briefly saw Mr. Woods very slowly beginning to take out his pistol. The time was getting near and I didn't have a second to spare.

During another lit moment, I looked back over to stage left and motioned for Kevin to walk toward me. The intro music was ending which only meant that it was about to be 8pm on the dot; my deadline.

Kevin saw my gesture and began walking over, the look on his face indicated that I may have needed something important and that he was there to tend to me. I looked back over to the front row and Mr. Woods was standing behind my mother making a hush gesture with his finger to his mouth while he had his pistol inches from her head. Mr. Sayer never broke eye contact with me and had a hungry smile on his face the whole time.

Back to my left, Kevin stepped closer and closer and in an instant, a flash of white, a flash of orange and all I, or anyone in the theater heard was a thunderous pop.

The stage lights came on and we began playing the intro to our first song of the set. I looked ahead and saw my mother covered in blood.

The first few rows were covered in blood.

Mr. Sayer and Mr. Woods, with shocked but impressed expressions on their faces, were covered in blood.

We were all covered in blood. I looked to my left and Kevin was nowhere to be seen.

Oh my god.

It fucking worked.

I was a genius!

You see, while mapping out our stage shows during rehearsals back in Hollywood, we specifically positioned pyro in certain spots of the stage to go off at particular times for added impact for our songs.

We wanted our pyro to be bigger and badder than any other band out there so we added a little something extra as far as gunpowder and dynamite for added oomph that could be potentially fatal for anyone standing too close but harmless for anyone more than a few feet away.

With my strict time limit and with my family's life at stake, I planned the whole intro of the show to be the murder of infamous concert promoter Kevin Reigns. I made sure he was stage left, exactly where I wanted him and had him take a few steps toward me so he would walk over exactly where one of our pyro canons would go off at the precise moment.

Kevin was virtually disintegrated which made for an even more bad ass show opening by raining blood all over us and the crowd. The best part was, nobody even saw it happen. Between the lights, and the sound, it happened within a millisecond. I informed Bob to tell Mr. Sayer what to expect during our show opening just to make sure I had all bases covered and I pulled it off.

The gig went incredibly well. We were fucking ferocious as a band and the crowd ate up every single note; especially my family and a very satisfied Mr. Sayer and Mr. Woods. I even caught them bobbing their heads to the music a few times.

It would probably be morbid to say it was one of the greatest moments of my life but taking everything into consideration and everything leading up to that point, it was purely euphoric.

We finished our set and the crowd wouldn't let us leave without an encore; so, we came back out and gave it to them. We ended up doing four encores that night. Our first show went monumentally. The whole venue was electric and we felt like the biggest band in the fucking world.

We finally ended our show with encore number four and headed back into our respective dressing rooms. Before I entered my room, a stage hand came up and asked me if I had seen Kevin anywhere to which I replied,

"Nope."

I closed the door to my dressing room, plopped down onto the leather couch and just let out the biggest sigh in the whole entire world. I had pulled it off. I was home free. I was finally able to enjoy myself.

The door swung open and my family rushed in. They were full of glee and happiness to see their Toby making it good in life and following his dreams. After hugs and kisses, I sent them on their way to go enjoy Kansas City and told them I would come visit them during the first break of my tour. We said our goodbyes and off they went.

Shortly after, Bob came in with a big smile on his face. He said,

"Dude, you are officially a fucking legend! On and offstage, a fucking legend!"

He continued his praises and gave me a big hug. I liked Bob. He genuinely seemed like a good dude who you just had to 'get' to understand fully. I was happy to have him as a pal for this journey.

Like clockwork, Mr. Sayer and Mr. Woods entered my dressing room as Bob left.

They both had an eerie smile on their face and sat me down.

"You exceeded in every way humanly possible, young man. We are beyond impressed. Enjoy your success and we will be seeing you soon seeing as we will have more work for you in the near future. But in the meantime, take a little breather, have some fun, and allow yourself to enjoy. Keep in mind, we will have eyes on you."

They both exited and I was left with my thoughts. I could have easily gone out and got some post show trim but felt I really needed to relax and just take a breather. It had been an insane couple of days and I deserved to take it easy. The next show was in two days so I had a chance to actually get some rest and mentally prepare for the rest of the tour.

15

ROCK STAR HITMAN

WE WERE A FEW weeks into the tour and the shows were going amazing. Our debut single was already certified gold and we were gaining huge momentum. But to be honest there were days when I missed the wholesome upbringing that I had in Delane.

Gone were the days of having real friends I could call and just do simple things with. Things like just going over to my buddy's house and listening to music, trading records, going out for a burger and just having a laugh. Instead, I had wayward 'yes men', wayward women, and my band; Bob wasn't even there for me to pal around with. I guess he may have just been a preliminary figure within The Agency's infrastructure.

For the record, I truly was ready for the big stage and the rock stardom because I prepared my whole life for that but my other job with The

Sayer Agency, no doubt, raped and certainly gnawed on my soul and desensitized my innocence.

While on tour, I would usually always try to get out of the hotel; especially on days off. There were a lot of great sites to see in America; things like the space needle in Seattle, The wharf in San Francisco, the big arch in St. Louis, and of course any beach anywhere, anytime.

Although I was terrible at geography, I at least knew where these things were and according to our tour schedule, was excited to be able to see them in person.

It felt nice to replace the murder and mayhem in my brain with innocent pleasures for a change. On a day off in Cincinnati, Ohio, I finally had a little time off and decided I should go fishing.

We were staying in a hotel a little bit out of town and the area felt very rural and reminded me of my hometown. I went down to the front desk and asked about renting a fishing pole, which they seemed to have. They even rented bikes. It had been a long time since I had gone on a bicycle ride.

I rented a bike and threw the fishing pole across my lap and headed down a small blacktop road which very quickly turned into a dirt road which led to a little lake in a swamp like area.

I found a nice spot but realized I had forgotten bait so I dug up an earthworm like we used to do back home; I then cast my line out and just relaxed.

I sat there lightly tugging on the line every so often to see if anything was going to be bite. After a few moments, I began to drift back to my days back in Delane. Then it really hit me just how far off the path I had really gotten. I had completely lost my innocence.

I had already put my family in danger and was responsible for the murders of a few people by that point. How would I bounce back from that mentally? I mean there I was just trying to relax on my day off, trying to fish, and I was already torturing myself about the things I had done and how things used to be. I wonder if Mr. Sayer had eyes on me in that particular moment.

I looked around the lake and it was dead calm aside from the sounds of nature. Was it paranoia? Or was it just life as I knew it? Was there a way out or was I in it for at least the next five years of my life? Was I experiencing buyer's remorse?

Man, I should have read that fucking contract.

As conflicted as I was mentally about everything, the shows were absolutely worth it. I just hated the fact that any free moment I got; I would drift back into feeling sorry for myself. I had fi-

nally made it but I couldn't even enjoy it proper-
ly. I guess there really was no such thing as a free
lunch.

I suddenly felt the urge to try and figure a
way out of my situation. Was there a way I could
get out of my contract? I mean seeing as The
Sayer Agency pretty much had corporate and legal America by the balls, was there a way I could
get out of it if I wanted to?

Suddenly, the chase for freedom replaced my
allure for rock stardom. I guess it was all true,
you always want something you can't have and,
in that moment, I sparked my yearning for freedom. Five more years and I was up for a renewal.
What did that even mean?

I sat there with my fishing pole and contem-
plated. How could I fall off the grid? Should I
fake my death? Relocate to some under the radar
third world village? Or was I just being an un-
grateful asshole?

I began to hate those contemplative moments.
I had everything in the palm of my hands and I
somehow wanted more? What was wrong with
me?

I needed to find a proper mental state and just
stick with it. A mental state that had no problem
with murder. A mental state that had no problem
with being a slave. A mental state that experienced little glimmers of joy like fishing on a

pond and just getting away from it all for a few hours.

I needed to learn how to enjoy myself again and decided just to live it up as much as I could. There was no escape from the situation and I needed to teach myself how to have fun again.

After a few hours of leisure and mental comfort, I packed up and headed back to the hotel. No bites, but it ain't the end of the world. It was time to get my head back into the music.

The band had become such a well-oiled machine and were into a routine. We were a band that played night after night that were just naturally great. Not only was it about playing tight as a musical group but it was also about the show being tight.

The lighting cues, the sound cues, the pyro, knowing where each of us were supposed to be on the stage as we moved from song to song, it was no longer guess work but was rather just an easy working part of the day.

Even my rapport with the audience night after night had started to become easy as I settled into my role as a real world-class bona fide rock star.

I tell you what though, I never heard pyro the same way ever again after the Kevin Reigns murder and I couldn't decide if that was a good feeling or bad feeling. I guess at the end of the day, all you can do is laugh at misfortune, right?

Every night on stage, our set list stayed pretty much the same. The only thing that would change was the city; so, me being terrible at knowing where I was at all times, always made sure that the name of the city we were playing was printed in big bold font on top of the setlist every night.

All it took was to fuck that up one time and you would lose the audience, unless you had an incredible come back like I did. We were performing in Indianapolis and for some reason I yelled out,

"Thank you, Omaha!"

Which was followed by a sea of boos. How could I confuse Indy with Omaha?! But no worries because I looked down at the setlist to see where the hell I was, chuckled, and quickly came back with,

"That's exactly what I would have said if you guys fucking sucked as a crowd but you don't; you rock, Indianapolis!"

The crowd then erupted with approval and from that, I think I had accidentally started a weird rivalry between Indianapolis and Omaha. Throughout the rest of the show, I would randomly hear people in the crowd yelling,

"Yeah! Fuck Omaha!"

It amazed me what you could get a group of people to believe in when you had them in the palm of your hands. But I had absolutely nothing against Omaha, obviously, it's a lovely place like everywhere else but sometimes you just gotta bounce back as best as you could in certain instances.

The hardest thing with my whole situation as a sort of 'rock star hitman' was keeping my head straight as I came into the venue every day knowing that I had my other job to worry about as well.

Once I hit that stage, the show just seemed to take over. It was just the long hours during the day that my mind would often drift back to the jobs I had done for The Sayer Agency as well as nervously awaiting the next assignment.

It had been a few weeks into the tour by that point, we had a break coming up, and I hadn't heard anything from Mr. Sayer at all. I truly hoped that they had forgot about me somehow.

But even with the things I had done for them up to that point, it was weird to think that both of my jobs, on the stage and off the stage, were technically performance driven.

There was an excitement leading up to it, there was adrenaline that would kick in, and once I locked into it, I sort of went into an alter ego and it was almost like I was on auto pilot while I was performing.

My goal was to try to remember the show that I did each night and yet somehow bury the memory of the dirty work I did for The Sayer Agency deep down inside me. In my way of mentally preparing for future Sayer work, I was hoping that my jobs for him would just blur together and just feel like any other Tuesday.

Tuesday.

That made me think about Robin. His Tuesdays were made up of some of the most debaucherously odd things that would mentally wound any normal human but for him, it was just a day that ended in 'y'.

I guess I could use that approach for what I did too. Poor Robin. But he played the game like anybody else and fell into his own abyss. Who knows how he would have been able to handle all of the dirty work if it was him that was doing it. But I guess everything happens for a reason, right?

At least that was what I kept telling myself.

16

DAPHNE

AS THE PLANE LANDED pulling into Omaha, we were met with a full fleet of black Chevrolet Suburbans on the tarmac to take us from the private jet over to the hotel. I wonder if Omaha had gotten wind of its new rival city of Indianapolis? I planned on tossing out the proverbial fishing line during the show to playfully find out.

The full brigade of our security team, dressed in sharp black suits, as well the staff of people whirling around us, whisked us in and out of the Suburbans into the hotel. It was always an exhilarating yet maddening feeling to get that kind of treatment from city to city.

After freshening up for a bit in my room, we were then escorted over to the venue for our sound check before the doors opened to let the fans in.

I couldn't help but be elated that all of our shows on that leg of the tour had been sold out. I sat in disbelief in my dressing room at how the entertainment business really worked. To see the likes of Michael Jackson, Frank Sinatra, and other notorious acts who somehow seamlessly worked their way to the top; it suddenly seemed to make sense. It was all thanks to The Sayer Agency.

I couldn't help but wonder that The Sayer Agency's mentality was somehow just a part we all played in selling our soul in exchange for fame and fortune. As if The Sayer Agency was truly the devil at the crossroads. Seeing as they have been around for hundreds of years, I could only assume that much.

At the same time, it fascinated me though. The whole concept of giving up your life for something you love in exchange for something you have to do but at the same time, that's life isn't it?

Throughout our day on the road, we would do a multitude of media and press events, usually which are press conferences where me and the band would sit at a table in a special activities room at a hotel or at the arena, and a dozen or so of the local press and media gathered up to ask us a multitude of questions while their tape recorders and cameras filmed our responses.

The idea being that a press conference was a sort of shotgun blast where a handful of questions would go out to multiple media outlets later that day or week.

During our stop in Seattle, Washington, on one of our afternoon press junkets at the hotel, I noticed a very striking woman who I learned was named Daphne. She was a freelance reporter who, on that particular day, was there to cover our show as well as our debut LP that we were touring in support of.

As soon as I walked into the room with the guys, we took our seats at the front of the room behind our long table and I took an immediate notice of her. Our eyes connected throughout the following thirty minutes at the press conference as we playfully flirted with each other from across the room.

Her height was around 5'8" and she had a beautiful chestnut shoulder length hair and gave off an aura of confidence and also that of inquisition. I was instantly intrigued and as soon as the press conference was over, I asked our press and media intermediary, Jacqueline, if she was able to arrange for me to have a drink at the bar with Daphne.

Jacqueline phoned me in my room about 15 minutes after the press conference and said that she had arranged for Daphne and I to grab a light snack and cocktail around 12:30 PM in the bar of the hotel.

It was a show day, so I had until about 3 PM before I had to depart from the hotel to the venue and begin our day's activities leading up to the concert.

I was as giddy as a teenager on their first prom date. I quickly cleaned up from the press conference, splashed some of my Calvin Klein cologne on me and made my way down the elevator to the restaurant bar in the hotel.

As I entered the room, I saw Daphne and Jacqueline engaged in conversation and light laughter. I already liked what I saw in Daphne as an engaging woman of intellect and intrigue.

As I approached the booth, Jacqueline took her cue that it was time for her to depart and leave me to strike up conversation with Daphne. Jacqueline offered an introduction between us although we had just been in the press conference together. It was unnecessary but provided a convenient handoff between us.

After Jacqueline escorted her way out, I reached for Daphne's hand to offer a light handshake, but not one that was in in anyway indicating that it was strictly about business. My heart fluttered as we connected and once again introduced myself as Sledge and she introduced herself as Daphne.

These were really unnecessary mild formalities as our eyes already made the deeper connection that indicated our hearts were both frolicking inside of us. I've had these kinds of encounters before but never at that level.

As much as I engaged in my after-show activities with the women who were a little looser and more willing to accommodate band members, like myself, who were passing through town for the evening; those one-night stands never developed into anything more than a simple lustful attraction.

But, in that moment, a woman sat before me who was elevating me to a higher level. If the other one-night stands were low hanging fruit, Daphne was clearly the star upon the tree.

As we engaged in our conversation, it really did feel like the first date of a teenage love affair and I sensed that there was going to be no after show "quickie" activity, nor was I in the mood for that with her.

What we had was truly a love interest that began to develop between us as we chatted, laughed and even playfully touched each other through our lunch, as if to say we wanted more of that physical connection and proximity. As they say, "you never know when love is going to walk through the door", and on that day in Seattle, that is exactly what happened.

After I drank my light beer and she took a few sips of her Cabernet wine, we shared a simple appetizer plate as we knew that it wasn't so much about the food as it was about making our connection.

I sheepishly asked for her phone number, which she was quick to offer. Her eyes said everything about her that I needed to know; that she was interested in me. She was enchanting and there was also a sensitive intrigue about her.

I sensed she was clearly not a rock 'n' roll girl of the night, but she wouldn't be sitting there with me if there wasn't something that she also found fascinating about me; to rub up a little bit against the unknown of the abyss. I was that abyss.

Conversely, Daphne elevated me to be on good behavior. I kept my language clean; I didn't talk about the rock 'n' roll road stories that I would normally share with people that I knew I was only going to be seeing for a few hours that day and probably never to be seen again.

My rock n' roll exploits were, in a sense, my badge of honor; a medallion of valiant service to all that I had given to rock and roll up to that point. But Daphne had my interest and she already had her hand on my heart.

I wasn't sure where it was going to go but I knew that it was just the beginning of something special together. For the first time in a long time,

I had the sudden feeling that everything was going to be all right.

It wasn't until after we gave a light kiss to the cheek and went our separate ways for the evening that I floated out of the hotel restaurant and back up to my room to pack up and head to sound check.

About two weeks after our initial meeting in Seattle, I offered for Daphne to fly down to visit me in Las Vegas. We had a two-night stand at Caesars Palace with a day off beforehand. The hotel was a fabulous luxury resort with five-star accommodations all around.

As much as I wanted to send the private jet to pick her up, clearly as a way to impress her, I knew that that would somehow raise a red flag with The Sayer Agency.

But Daphne was a lady, not a little girl. She clearly made her own money and was a woman on her own two feet. So just the mere suggestion from me to come visit, she quickly offered to buy her own plane ticket and be on her own itinerary.

I loved her independence because I knew if I were to buy a first-class ticket for her on my credit card, it may have left a paper trail that The Sayer Agency could one day trace if they ever audited my personal expenditures, which I was quite certain they were already doing.

Upon her arrival at Caesars Palace, I instantly fell in love with Daphne all over again. Our late-night phone calls during the previous two weeks were deep and intense.

I realized that as a young man in my early 20s, investing into a real romantic relationship was not an area of my life that I ever really put much time into. In fact, outside of a few girls I dated in high school back in Delane, Daphne was my first real foray into having what might actually become a real girlfriend.

My career was on track and I was starting to make quite a bit of money, so the distractions of a girlfriend getting in the way of my music career were mostly behind me now.

However, I was quickly learning that the one downside of the rock star life was that while the world was my oyster and women practically threw themselves at me wherever I went; sex was a very different animal from romance.

What I was feeling with Daphne was a real kinship and a heartfelt friendship with another woman. So much so, that my interest in the usual after-hours parties following the concerts immediately came to a halt.

Suddenly my interests with her were much greater than just flirtatious conversations. I was no longer interested in just finding the next girl or after show party favors.

After three whirlwind days in Las Vegas together, doing everything from fine dining to stepping into an occasional after hours show on the strip, it was clear that Daphne and I were an item. Because she was a grown-up, I sensed that she clearly knew about my lifestyle on the road yet she never asked questions.

One of the most difficult and challenging parts of my lifestyle was that everyone thought they knew a rock star's life from what they saw on the stage, but no one really knew what actually went on in one's mind and heart once the spotlight fades and are left all alone in a hotel room.

Add to that the double life I was already living between being a rock star by night and my lingering day job with The Sayer Agency; the last thing I needed was another double life with late night parties and girls after the show while trying to procure a proper and romantic relationship with Daphne.

Fortunately, she didn't ask, so therefore I didn't have to tell. In more ways than one it was the ideal relationship.

We kept our conversations going via phone and with my break in the tour approaching, I decided to split that time up between spending it with her and my family, whom I promised I would see during the two-week break during the tour cycle.

Daphne and I both agreed to meet in a secluded rental cabin in Colorado so that we could be completely isolated from the outside world allowing her and I to enjoy each other's company with absolutely zero distractions from my lifestyle or hers.

We played our final show before our break and like all the others before it, was completely sold out and was a huge success on all fronts.

The one thing in the back of my mind that I buried away for some time was The Sayer Agency and their plans for me. I hadn't heard a single thing from anyone in that camp whatsoever. Not since the first show of the tour. Maybe all I had to do was a few assignments at the beginning of each tour? Who knows? Either way, my main focus was Daphne and our cabin getaway in the mountains.

I arrived at the cabin and the landscape was so beautiful it almost looked fake. As if it were just a painted backdrop of blue skies and snow-capped mountains. As I pulled into the front of the cabin, I saw that Daphne had already arrived. The butterflies in my stomach began fluttering. I genuinely couldn't wait to see her and progress our budding love for each other.

I stuck the key into the cabin door and slowly opened it ajar. My whole life in the clouds up to that point had turned into an evil hurricane the second my eyes fell upon what was inside that cabin.

17

IT'S ALL A MEANS TO AN END

IT WAS LIKE A horrific reunion of sorts. Mr. Sayer, Bob, and Mr. Woods were standing behind Daphne who was gagged, tied to a chair, and bleeding. Tears dropped from her eyes the second she saw me. My heart filled with rage and confusion. I dropped to me knees,

"What the fuck is going on here?! Why?!"

I screamed with every ounce of being.

With his signature devilish smile, Mr. Sayer said,

"You really should have read your contract, Toby. The whole contract. You should know better than to be getting into serious relationships and attempting to schedule secret rendezvous behind our back."

My ignorance had gotten the best of me again but I couldn't even attempt to think straight in that moment. I knew things were too good to be true the way they were going with the tour and with Daphne. I knew something had to give at some point. I replied with,

"What are you going to do with her? Just set her free and I will never contact her again. I promise. You have to believe me."

Mr. Woods smiled and Mr. Sayer went on to say,

"Oh, it's not as simple as that, young man. You see we have to abide by tradition within The Agency and in tradition, misery truly loves company."

"You see, for the five years that you are contracted to us, you are not allowed to have personal relationships, children, etc. anything that could possibly get in the way of how we need things taken care of."

"With that said, you are forced to 'handle' your distraction with extreme prejudice. You belong to us, Toby, and there is nothing you can do about it."

He then motioned for Mr. Woods to hand me a pistol.

I yelled, "No! I will not harm this woman and neither will you!"

Mr. Sayer laughed,

"That's perfectly fine to think that way, Sledge, it really is, but you need to remember something; the stakes are always high and when we are involved, the stakes always are just a little bit higher."

Mr. Sayer then motioned to Mr. Woods who proceeded to open up a bedroom door and brought out my family one by one, also tied, gagged, and bleeding. My heart sank even more.

Mr. Sayer continued,

"So, it's quite simple, Toby. Either you kill Daphne, or we kill your family. Or you could take an alternate way out and we can just kill all of you. Oh, and if it helps, we can tell you that Daphne was a cold-hearted child murderer, or a drug trafficker, or drug dealer or whatever else we told you to make sure you had enough balls and motivation to handle our prey."

I was stunned,

"What are you talking about?"

Mr. Sayer continued,

"You see, Toby, Sledge, or whatever the hell your name is, we control the narrative. We control your life. Consider this your graduation and promotion within The Agency. No more kid gloves."

"Who's to say that Ronald Kovis was actually a good-hearted family man who just placed a few bad bets with the wrong people?"

"Who's to say that Kevin Reigns was actually a decent human being and great concert promoter but just rubbed us the wrong way?"

"Who's to say that Phil was actually a genuinely wonderful human being that just got too close to you?"

"That's up to you to decide. Now, take the gun and handle your situation. Oh, and don't even think about harming either of us. There will be a bounty on your head so big that your own reflection will be trying to murder you."

It was one of the worst moments of my life. I had finally started feeling feelings again and thought that everything wasn't so bad. Even though I had to murder a few people who deserved to be murdered here and there, but with what I had become privy to information wise, I didn't even know what was real and what wasn't anymore.

How was I supposed to be able to live with myself? It crossed my mind to just grab the gun and off myself so I didn't have to watch these mad men kill the love of my life and family. What could I do? Was there anything I could do?

I looked around and there was literally nothing to be done. I closed my eyes as hard as I could to try and wake up from that awful nightmare but nothing was working. Nothing could prepare me for what had to be done. I felt my brain breaking. I felt the need to just scream. To just die. How was I supposed to take someone's life that didn't deserve to die?

I then felt a gun being put into my hands and Mr. Sayer whispered in my ear,

"It's all a means to an end, boy."

I was transported back to my first kill at the slaughterhouse. That poor cow, Grace, for whom I humanized and felt for. Maybe I was just a cold-hearted killer after all? Maybe it was who I was destined to be? A murderer who moonlighted as a successful rock star. Not the other way around.

Perhaps I needed to just bite the bullet and send Daphne on her way to whatever the afterlife may hold. We lived in an awful world anyway, maybe she would be better off?

Oh god. Here I was trying to rationalize murder again, but what else was I supposed to do? I couldn't do anything but go with the flow.

My eyes were still shut but the emotional pain shooting through my whole body prevented me from being able to stand up. All I could hear was Daphne pleading through her gag for help. All I could see was darkness.

Then all of a sudden, I felt peace and comfort knowing that, one day, my awful life would end and that it was better to have loved than to have never have loved at all. I opened my eyes, stood up, and said,

"Okay, Mr. Sayer. I'll do it."

He smiled and said,

"Good boy."

I then pointed my gun at Daphne's head from where I was standing which was a good few feet away. I closed my eyes and gently began to squeeze the trigger.

It felt like an eternity, just waiting for that thunderous pop of the bullet leaving the barrel and murdering my girlfriend.

After what felt like a lifetime, I finally heard the pop.

I couldn't bear to open my eyes.

Dead silence fell upon the whole cabin as the shot echoed throughout the mountains.

Then all I began to hear was laughter. Sinister laughter no doubt. I slowly opened my eyes and saw Mr. Sayer, Bob, and Mr. Woods all laughing at me. I looked down and saw that Daphne was unharmed along with my family. I couldn't understand what had just happened.

Mr. Sayer, almost falling over with laughter pointed down at my gun and said,

"Look, you fool!"

At the end of the barrel of the gun was a flag sticking out that said "Bang" on it. It was a joke gun. What the fuck was going on?

Mr. Sayer and his crew proceeded to fall over from laughter, even Mr. Woods was losing it. Then Daphne began nervously laughing along with my family. I felt like I was going absolutely insane.

Finally, Mr. Sayer composed himself, though still chuckling, and said,

"You actually thought we were that cold-hearted man? Holy shit!" What was happening here?

He continued,

"Sledge, we just needed to see if you would do it and you, sir, are one cold hearted son of a bitch! We don't care that you have a girlfriend! We just needed to see how dedicated you were to our company and with the help from Daphne and your family, you passed with flying colors!"

I was stunned.

He continued,

"You see it isn't us you have to worry about. We do have a rival company who probably would hold your girlfriend and family hostage and probably rape and kill them all in front of you too; The Ingram company. They're the cold-hearted assholes that we are trying to eradicate."

I couldn't believe it. It was one big prank! I asked,

"What about the people I've killed? Were they really bad people?"

Mr. Sayer still laughing, slightly nodded and contradictingly said,

"I don't know I guess that's up to you to decide!"

Him and his crew continued to laugh. He then said,

"I will tell you this though,"

He regained his composure fully and looked me dead in the eye and became the most serious I had ever seen him,

"If you ever fuck us over, you can bet your life that this scenario will happen again and there won't be any fake guns. Consider this The Sayer Agency showcasing its dominance."

"You have been warned and are now prepared for any situation that you may find yourself in. Your family and Daphne will be instructed to never speak of this moment again or otherwise will face dire consequences."

He then tossed a portfolio toward me and continued,

"Here are your next assignments. I suggest you enjoy your two-week break because when we kick back off, you're going international and there's a whole new breed of evil overseas that you haven't even seen yet. Rest up, Sledge. It's game on."

I was completely mind fucked by The Agency. I was happy at the fact that Daphne and my family were safe but at the same time, wow.

From that point forward I knew that I needed to keep a mental separation from everything. I needed to be able to walk away from anything and anyone in thirty seconds flat if I felt the heat coming from around the corner.

I was being twisted and turned emotionally in so many different directions that I could barely see straight. It must have been what they did in the military. They'd beat you down to nothing and build you back up into a stone-cold killing machine.

Somehow, my wits have survived the situation and I needed to get focused on Europe. If all the world's a stage then I guess I have no choice but to kill it either way.

EPILOGUE

SO, THERE I WAS, on a train heading to a small town outside of Belgrade, Serbia. On my way to make the next drop off; a little detour before the next gig. All I had on me was my guitar case, my duffel bag, and the thought swimming around in my head,

Was this all worth it?

That thought had been there since the beginning; just knocking itself around in my brain, slowly getting more violent, psychologically as well as physically.

How many times did I need to wash the blood out of my stage clothes before I realized that the price of fortune and fame wasn't worth transporting a severed head in a fucking duffel bag?

How many times did I need to show up to a man's hotel, knife in hand, to brutally send a "personal message" to him and his "people"?

I fucking hated it when they'd make me use a knife

It was so damn messy.

I got their logic though; it was quiet and it made a strong point, but they weren't the ones who had to clean all the shit up and arrange what was left of them methodically so it made some kind of dramatic sense to the people who would discover him.

So many questions for a no questions asked gig.

It drove me insane.

One more question,

Was I going to be able to shower before the gig?

Would I be able to wash the brain matter and skull off me before the show?

Oh yeah. The show.

It was ramping up to be a good one that night. Sold out. Twenty-five thousand people, all there for me cheering, screaming my name; that beautiful fucking noise.

I loved that shit.

The adrenaline and drugs running through my veins the second our intro music would start.

The prospect of pointing out to my guitar tech which blondes and how many to give, what we call, a "slut pass" to; for after gig festivities.

That "white noise" feeling in the middle of our set where everything would just go into a slow-motion flash where the music, the fans, the drugs and the band culminated into a fever pitch of euphoria.

Shit.

Thinking about it, maybe it wasn't so bad.

Maybe I just needed to stop thinking about things and take another hit. One hit closer to that beautiful white noise that made contract murder all worth the trouble.

I needed to stay focused.

I wanted it and I had it.

I needed to be grateful.

Okay.

Enough bitching.

I had a job to do.